THE LISTENERS

THE LISTENERS

A novel by Leni Zumas

🐚 Tin House Books
Portland, Oregon & New York, New York

Published by Tin House Books, Portland, Oregon, and New York, New York

Distributed to the trade by Publishers Group West, 1700 Fourth St., Berkeley, CA 94710, www.pgw.com

Library of Congress Cataloging-in-Publication Data

Zumas, Leni, 1972-

The listeners : a novel / by Leni Zumas. — 1st U.S. ed.

p. cm.

ISBN 978-1-935639-29-9 (trade paper) — ISBN 978-1-935639-30-5 (ebook)

1. Young women—Family relationships—Fiction. 2. Sisters—Death--Fiction. 3. Neurasthenia—Fiction. 4. Families—Psychological aspects—Fiction. 5. Domestic fiction. 6. Psychological fiction. I. Title.

PS3626.U43L57 2012

813'.6—dc22

2012002068

First U.S. edition 2012

Printed in the USA

Interior design by Jakob Vala and Diane Chonette

www.tinhouse.com

For Diana and Greg
and in memory of our uncle Tony

THE CLERK HAD two thumbs on his left hand. One was normal, the other a nub of flesh and nail sprouting from the foot of the normal one. Out of politeness I tried not to look at it, but every time I bought cigarettes there came a moment when he turned and I could watch the second thumb. It seemed to possess a kind of intelligence. A wise baby tentacle with powers of its own.

I asked how he was doing.

"Half a damn foot more tonight," he said, "if you believe the radio."

The sidewalks were hard little white seas. Built on a swamp, our city was not good at handling winter. Twice as long to walk to the subway, and the train platform slick with melt. The man beside me was wet-coughing. When he spat into his sleeve, I shut my eyes. *And hold your breath when the doors open or the tunnel germs will get into your lungs and grow like lichen. We are all the way under the earth. We are how many leagues down?*

Snowflakes salted the early dark, the street a white field cut by tires and boots. A siren, laughter, throbs of music from the takeout. Our mother thought my brother's apartment was too loud, not guessing that Riley used the noise for company. Snow was an ear feather. Airplanes blinked in the sky. A car radio said a car bomb had killed three American soldiers, and the buzzer threw blue veins up the wall.

"Hello," crackled his little intercom voice.

What the dickens was he wearing? A sackcloth over pale denim, and canvas sneakers—I was regularly impressed by the ghastliness of his wardrobe. The apartment was neat as a new pin, or a German barracks. Couch pillows all plump and straight, can of dried flowers in the corner, table with nothing on it but the expensive type of candle. It made me want to take a dump on the floor.

"Nice dirndl," I said.

"Shut up, thank you."

"Took a new one?"—nodding at a tiny frame hung up, a prune-eyed woman in hectic scarves.

Riley smiled at his sneakers. "Yeah that's Mrs. Jones from downstairs."

"The fake fortune-teller?"

"*You* don't know if she's fake," my brother said quietly.

We were late but safe together: the meal couldn't start without us. Mert would have fussed a little over the table, gotten out place mats. Lawyers and salesclerks, custodians and telemarketers, all rumpled from the day—we sidestepped them. As usual I imagined the destinations of strangers to be firmer than my own. They all had real places to be, where real things happened. A bike messenger knocked Riley practically to the ground, but the poor slow flower wouldn't think to give him the finger. My brother was a baby monk. He blinked a lot. He worked in a windowless office twenty feet below street level, and no matter the creepy chief or the loud-chewing receptionist or the smell from the break-room icebox, Riley loved it in that bunker. For eight hours a day his head was soft and loose, with tasks to absorb it, thick walls and controlled temperature and the breath of other archivists.

Out of a coffee shop drifted a tinny song.

"Come on," he said.

"Hold it," I said. *Them*? One song on rotation at a corporate-bean megalith, you never needed to work again. And the members of that wormy outfit should've had to work until the very hour of their deaths—

"What's wrong?"

"Ten-foot-talls," I hissed.

"Quinn, the bus… come on…"

We ran, in our fashion. Neither of my lungs was in full operation, and Riley had virtually no muscle mass.

"You need to quit smoking," he accused as we sank down. "And what's a ten-foot-tall?"

"Bleh," I said.

We conjectured about the evening menu, agreeing it better not be veal, or Cornish hens that weren't cooked all the way. We recalled the night Riley had complained about the blood and I said, Yeah, this is foul fowl! and Fod said nothing and Mert threw down a bowl of broccoli, which clattered but did not break. I am never cooking dinner for this family again, she announced. Then she sat, shook out her napkin, and forked a dripping red bite. Enough theatrics, Fod said. You think these are theatrics? she whispered—the whisper of trying not to scream. I refuse to prepare food night after night for people who do not appreciate it. But you're not *really* going to stop, I reasoned. Believe me, our mother snapped, I am.

"I vote for brisket," said Riley now.

"No, fish; and some kind of nutritious sea vegetable." I added, "Oh to be on the road, when all you ingested was gummy bears and locally popular beverages."

"Yeah," he said. Riley was a good-sport listener: he'd nod and murmur, the whole while thinking his own thoughts in a private chamber. I told the same stories over and over, and he never had the heart to point it out. *Like when we picked up that deaf hitchhiker in Oregon. Like when we got attacked by feral turkeys in Ohio.*

The house on Observatory Place was a meek square of brick and blue wood, pots of dead geraniums on the porch, walnut branches a-scratch at the upper windows. I coughed to disguise my huffing from the hill, a hill that in high school had not challenged me at all.

Riley slapped me on the back. "By the way."

"Yeah?"

"Where's my twenty?" he said.

"Um, what?"

"From last week. You said you were getting paid today."

I coughed louder, wiped my mouth. "You are correct, sir."

He paused on the porch steps, waiting.

"Let me just find my wallet," I told him.

Indoors he said, "This looks great" because Mert had gone to the trouble of candles. Pork chops and mashed parsnips and brussels sprouts and a saucer, for me, of grilled tofu. Riley told about his horrible boss at the archives and how a coworker had yelled Lawsuit! when the boss stroked her cheek. When it was my turn to report, I poured another wine and said, "Same as usual, business very bad."

"Might be time to look elsewhere," Fod said in the fake-casual voice.

"I can't ditch Ajax," I reminded him.

Mert, who was ashamed to have a daughter in her midthirties working in a bookstore (a used one, at that) cut in: "Squidlings, how about helping me with some cleaning next weekend? All that junk in the basement, there's so much that really should be tossed..."

I spooned a splotch of parsnip. Riley said okay.

"Thank you, Coyote—Saturday morning?"

I said, "You're not getting rid of any of *her* stuff, though, right?"

Mert said, "Want to come by at nine thirty?"

I mouthed at him, *Don't throw her stuff away.*

"I have a funny thing," Riley said when the silence had gotten long.

"Yes, pettle?"

"Well, I was in the supermarket looking at peanut butter and I had to read all the different labels because you know how most of them are so sugary but don't need to be because—"

"Get *on* with it," I said.

"Okay so I'm there, and I don't think I looked particularly gloomy but this woman who I now remember as a wizened gypsy but could have been just a regular woman comes up and hands me a pamphlet. It had an orange sunset and big swirly letters and said: COMFORT FOR THE DEPRESSED. Take it, she said, it will help you."

"That's disturbing," said Fod.

"No, it's *funny*. All I was thinking about was peanut butter!"

"You *do* look depressed, though," I said.

"Now, now—"

"Admit it, Mert, his default expression is one of gentle despair."

"He has a very handsome face," she said.

"But it's not exactly merry or bright."

Throughout my brother's life, gas-station attendants, ticket takers, and college professors had urged him: Come on, smile, it can't be *that* bad!

Fod grunted, "Who has anything to be merry about? The United States government is torching people's human rights on a daily basis."

"Oh *okay*—"

"Don't give me that dismissive crap," he told our mother. "You can turn your face to the wall, but that wall might get blown up by an AGM-114 Hellfire. Know why they're called Hellfires? It's an abbreviation. The official term for these delightful contraptions is *Helicopter-launched fire-and-forget.* Oops, pardon me, dreadful sorry, these missiles are so easy to use I *forgot* that I sent one into your child's face yesterday—"

"Thank you *Masterpiece Theater.* So Riley, what did you say to the woman at the store?"

"Nothing. I mean, I probably said thanks."

"I would've told her to shove that sunset up her poon," I remarked, reaching for the wine.

THE FAMILY WAS five, its children born in the 1970s in a middle-income suburb of a medium East Coast city. The father was a tenured professor of organic chemistry and the mother taught English literature as an adjunct lecturer at the same university. They had met in graduate school, conceived the first kid not long after, and married three months before her birth. The middle child felt wholly a girl. The youngest wanted to be a girl because his sisters were. The oldest hovered between girl and boy, both, neither.

The middle said: "Close your eyes so the germs don't get in. This train has germs that love the eyes. They crawl through the whites and gnaw to the brain and swim down your blood to the heart."

"But I want to see," said the youngest, "how it looks when we come out of the dark—when we're up on stilts."

"That's not for a while," said the middle. "*Close them.*"

The youngest did.

"It's worse to be gnawed in the heart than in the brain." The middle lowered her voice away from the parents, who sat at the far end of the subway car. The oldest and the middle were starting to like to escape them in public, and the youngest, if he had to choose, always chose his sisters.

"What does the brain matter," whispered the middle, "compared with the heart?"

The oldest opened her eyes before she was supposed to. She saw black walls rush past the glass. She watched a guy drum on a denim thigh some private song. Being alone with noise in your ears and an army-colored jacket and your hair all crazy was so much better than riding home with your family from the museum.

"You can look now," said the middle when the train had come up out of the ground. "Our municipal subway system," she announced, "started being built in 1969 and was finished in 1976."

The youngest asked if during construction there had been explosions.

Yes was the answer. And accidents. Many deaths.

"Next stop, pettles!" called the mother.

The oldest wished the parents would get off without them. She wanted to ride until sleepy and sleep until the train had reached a station she'd never been to, in a country she'd never seen.

After the train, the walk, the removal of red and blue coats, they brought sloshing cups downstairs and stood a lit candle on the basement floor. The cherry juice made their teeth black, their tongues vampire. "If while at sea you got a fatal case of calenture—*a distemper*," read the middle from her notebook, "*peculiar to sailors in hot climates, wherein they imagine the sea to be green fields, and will throw themselves into it, if not restrained*—would you rather drown alive or be shot by the captain?"

"Shot," said the oldest.

"Drown," said the youngest, "because then you might not drown but have a dolphin save you."

The middle shook her head. "This is in a part of the ocean," she said, "where dolphins went extinct. Now do you guys know about the different ides?" She gleamed her I've-done-my-research smile, which according to their mother was not very becoming. "March is famous," the middle explained, "as the month when ides should be wared of, but many perilous things have taken place on the fifteenth of February as well. For instance: on this day in 1961, flight 548 crashed in Belgium, killing seventy-three people, including every figure skater on the U.S. Olympic team. On the ides of February of *this very year*"—she paused for effect—"the drilling rig *Ocean Ranger* sank during a vicious storm off the Newfoundland coast, and eighty-four rig workers died.

"But good things happened too," she went on, "like Susan B. Anthony from the coin was born on this day in 1820. And Sir Ernest Shackleton popped from the womb on this day in 1874. He saved every last sailor from an icy death, although the sled dogs had to be killed. And on February 15, 1564, Galileo Galilei came into the world. He was the first to see craters on the moon."

TEN YEARS AGO, a man called Ajax who wore wooden jewelry gave me a job out of sheer kindness, and I'd worked at his bookstore ever since. I had never been the biggest reader, which worried me at first, but I learned to pony up convincing answers to customers on the shortest of notices. I could refer to writers so quickly and slurrily that the customer would nod along no matter what I was saying. If an aficionado wanted to have an actual literary conversation, my eyelids would droop and I'd fiddle with the calculator until Ajax swooped in, with his genuine knowledge, to rescue.

At lunch hour we had strawberry soda and cocoa patties from the Jamaican grill. Ajax bent over his newspaper while I paced the linoleum aisles. Our little graveyard lay in the shade, its shelves aburst with stories, bins packed with remains, bunting slung limp from the ceiling, and for hours at a time, for days on end, nary a customer. It was an improbable location for a bookstore, out here among the office blocks and furniture outlets and restaurants full at lunchtime of trembling chrome-haired ladies. Each stack of pages in its cardboard sleeve was a house, and in each house things happened without anyone knowing. The houses were dead because no one would read them again. We had our regulars and the mail orders, but both were measly.

A spider clung to the net of flesh between my thumb and finger; my other hand flicked it off and pounded it flat on the scarred counter.

Two boys strutted in, cold-faced sparks, their garb a tattered skin on spitefully thin limbs. It was a good thing their assflesh had been hacked away, or had never grown in the first place, because the britches didn't have room for it. They were not so much pants as denim harnesses, sliced low, grazing the pubic bone. I had once relied on my own skinniness to pull off that kind of look.

The taller spark asked, "You got any books by the guy who went to jail for building a half-pipe on Indian burial grounds?"

I stared at him.

"Do you?"

"He only wrote one, and it's garbage." (In fact it probably was.)

"Well do you have it?"

"You might consider looking on the memoir wall."

"Whatever, lady."

Lady? Neither stripling had removed his fly-eye glasses. *Lady?* And now a girl, even younger than the boys, attractive in a cake-mix sort of way, strolled in.

School must've just gotten out. Both waxy heads turned; they appraised her clinically as she leaned into the new arrivals table, shrugging off her pink wool coat.

She left without buying anything. So did the sparks. The silence in the store was so huge I could hear every twist and shimmer of ring in my ears. I flicked on the radio, which stayed at talk stations—Ajax honored my no-music policy. Thought it was stupid, but honored it.

Those kids should've known who I was. Even after all this time.

Narcissus was a flower but was also a boy. The boy loved the sight of himself and so he loved water. The problem with Narcissus: oneself was only of limited interest. Sometimes, to ward off the tedium of Quinn, I went into the heads of people I knew. I was Geck; I was Riley; I was my smarter sister. I listened to their conversations. Watched them watch TV or make toast. I liked borrowing their heads.

I popped open a red can of chips, closed my eyes at the factory taste dear to me since childhood. The radio was listing war-death statistics, so I turned it back off. Silence, buzzing. For three seconds, the most I could stand, I made myself pretend I was deaf. This was how it felt: the flat hush unbroken by a single noise other than the hum in my canals. Riley would have to learn sign language.

"**THE TORPEDO IS** a fish that if you touch while it's alive, even with a long stick, your hand will go numb, perhaps forever. But if it's dead you can eat it." The middle looked up from her notebook. "So what would you do if the king commanded you to kill one?"

"Shoot it with a rifle," said the oldest.

"Ask the king," said the youngest, "if he could please command someone else."

THE BAR WAS its usual self, smudged mirror and crack-vinyled banquettes, idleness warming the air. Sparklers dressed to the teeth were chattering at every table. My spot on the end stool had been commandeered by some fellows who had the look of a band about them: their outfits were variations on a pinstriped theme, and their droopy haircuts matched, and their number was four. The one most likely to be the singer (shiniest hair, bonniest face) was telling the others: "I'm just gonna book it to South America, if so. No way I stick around to get slaughtered on a camel track." He swung his polished locks, tipped beer into his mouth.

"Me neither," said the one who, fattest, would have been the drummer.

"Yeah, fuck *that* they can't institute a *draft* it's the twenty-first century!" added the bass player, dumbest.

Their eye-corners were unwrinkled, thighs spindly, they were killable. I watched them in the hot sand, these dapper four, a row of pinstriped puppies jerking and flopping in the bullet spray.

Mink wiped the zinc and chewed a lime, worrying its pulp for last juices. She was sweating hard. She was letting the other girl fetch my drinks. When did she ever do that? Normally she was a good lieutenant, always had the new drink ready before being asked.

"They try to draft me, I'll shoot my toe off," declared the drummer. "How you like me *now*?"

When Mink drew near I said: "Bad day or something?"

She turned. "I bounced three checks."

"Oops."

"Ninety dollars in fees."

"Re-up *ici*, madam!" shouted the singer.

"One second." Mink hunched and unhunched her shoulders, slow; then bent to serve.

The singer looked over at me. Kept looking. I decided to be flattered.

"Hey," he said. "You're that—I mean you were in—I mean you used to play around here, right?"

"I did," I said.

"I *thought* so." He took a pull from the glass Mink had set down. "There's an old poster of y'all up at WMUC. I have a show."

"Congratulations."

"So this is totally weird, because I just saw another guy from your outfit. Today. A few fucking hours ago. And now I see you."

"How come you didn't see *her*?" I said, pointing at Mink. "She was in it, too."

The singer looked. Shrugged. "Time is a hammer.

Anyway, for some reason I thought that guy died. Didn't one of you, like, die?"

"No," I said.

"Oh. Sorry, I don't know why I thought that." He swallowed more beer. "I kept thinking when I saw him—this was on the subway, right—isn't that guy dead? And really tall, by the way. What is he, six four?"

Geck was not tall.

"I think you saw someone else," I said.

"No, he had the exact same face as on the poster. And the hair. Old-fashioned, you know? Like, a black flop."

Geck was blond.

I fretted my wristband. Pluck, snap, pluck, snap. Stretched the rubber far enough to break. When the bracelet had first been assigned to me by the good doctor, I didn't intend to use it, until I discovered that it worked. It brought my brain back to itself. If terror, crack band brutally hard. If dread, flick elastic and focus on pinch: dread gone.

CAM DIDN'T COUNT as a ghost; he was perfectly alive. I had never doubted that he was, though in ten years I hadn't heard hide nor hair.

He had been good at every school subject.

He had loved American cola.

He had opposed the shaving or waxing of pubic hair, believing nether-whisker removal to be decorative where no decoration belonged. "The cock is an *organ*," he once said. "It's not like you're going to dress your liver up in a bonnet."

SNOW IMPROVED MY ragged neighborhood: the scrawny
trees went gentle against the falling white, and each fin-
gerwide housefront appeared to be a holder of secrets. A
gray cat looked up, flakes collecting on its lashes. Hello,
cat. I turned my key, climbed the black stairs, wondered
if his eyes would catch too much cold in them. Poured
a glass of half cherry juice, half whiskey, and drank it
in two swallows. My octopus watched from the couch.
It was too warm in here, the first-floor stereo too loud.
Pulled off my glimmie and drenched socks. Thermostat
had been jacked—it was hard to breathe. I stomped on
a loose board. Should open a window. The music tightened to a tunnel, sharpening, grinding, and my eyes
had too much water in them: the couch reeled in jelly:
I needed to sit. Where was Octy? I would sit with him.
First open a window, then sit. First sit, then open—? I
couldn't hear anything except wind raking the hairs. The
floor came up through the water to meet me.

And I woke up in the bells. They fell straight down from the cathedral. The news of Cam was still there—I prodded my throat, where it had lodged. *He had the exact same face as on the poster.* But it wasn't him. Couldn't be. Pinstriped Jacket had been mistaken.

It was my day off, and I wished it weren't. *You have a brain, why don't you use it?* My brother too sat for way too long at windows, stayed in his apartment for stretches of more than twenty-four hours. I, at least, was mostly able to fake it, but Riley was all bashfulness, a scuttler at life's hem. Had he ever had sex? Of *course*, he was three decades old! But had he? His bedsheets were decorated with ladybugs, and how could that teen-friar body dare tangle up with another? It was mortifying to picture him naked, all bone and hair, no ass, eyes bulby with terror, skin freckled and moled—a chalky hide like my own, inherited from Belfast, Cardiff, Manchester.

I radiated a burrito and spooned on salsa. Stared at the swollen lump under its cheerful sauce, fat-drenched blood slowing and hardening. "It's fine," I said out loud. But that whitish chicken-yellow smell of raw fat in the gash—I breathed, breathed, waited for new air in my mouth. Burrito into trash.

It had been a long time since I noticed the blood in my food. Years, maybe. But the blood seemed to be back.

Never fear. I flipped on the plastic machine for a round of my newest game, wherein the streets of an island city were strewn with poked corneas, wrung necks, and slit throats. Nighttime always. Knives and guns were the standard, but once you accumulated enough points you got to use poison-dipped arrows or a laser that from a hundred feet could stop a heart.

On my street, I was one of two white residents, the other a hunchback elder who slabbed on clown-blush for her trips to the store—unless there happened to be some white invalids or white serial killers who never showed their faces. Two Thumbs handed me a new pack and nodded, businesslike. I wished he would say something, even a weatherly remark, because I liked his voice, so squeaky for so jumbo a guy.

"Busy today?"

He shrugged.

I stole a look at the stub; its teeny nail was clean.

Crossing into the next neighborhood (whiter, sprucer) I passed a spark whose mouth was half gone under a chunk of hair. Then I saw them: not one poster, not two, but twenty. Their faces marched the whole way down the block. These mooncalves were never supposed to get big; in fact, they'd claimed not to want to. Their creepy little efforts to make art without bowing to the marketplace had annoyed me but had also been a comfort: they would never be famous. Yet now they were everywhere—piped loud into coffee chains, ten feet tall on construction barriers. The singer, Jupiter, had lost major weight since last I saw him. Where have *you* been hiding yourself? he'd said and I muttered something about a new project I was assembling, and he said anytime we wanted to open for them we were welcome to. You guys helped us so much when we were starting out, he added, palming a supermarket cantaloupe as if he could have learned something from how it felt.

We did not help you intentionally, I'd wanted to say.

Cam had hated them too.

I wondered if there might be an official name for the syndrome where you feel like you have to leave the house or you will die, but then, after ten minutes of being outside, all you want is to go back in.

Back at the ranch I was greeted by two pieces of mail. One was from my landlord, memo-style: *Your final warning.* Once again it was past the fifteenth and I had not paid this month's, and he wanted me to know that he could start eviction proceedings if it happened one more time. But he was all bluster and no organization. I had been here long enough not to fear him.

The other was a letter from Carlton E. Shutz, Wilson High School alum:

> Here's hoping you all are happy, healthy, and thriving in every way—that your kids are eating their vegetables without insisting on the airplane-spoon trick every time; that your spouse puts the cap back on the toothpaste; that your neighbors' skateboarding stunts don't start before ten on Sundays; that your jury duty was brief, interesting and came out the right way; that your team has a

good shot at the Final Four, and that even if your team has no shot, that your pool picks have an uncanny, lucky feel to them; that your running times and mortgage rates are down and your bowling scores and IRAs are up; and that you're still (happily) surprised every so often by the world despite our more than a third-of-a-century worth of experience in it.

It went on to ask for a donation to Wilson's alumni fund. I didn't remember Carlton E. Shutz and I did not know we had turned fifty-five instead of thirty-five. Mortgage rates? Cap back on the *toothpaste*? Or by thirty-five did pretty much everyone have an IRA?

"**IF A *DRACUNCULUS*** got under your skin, what would you do?"

"A *quoi*?"

The middle read sternly from her notebook: "*A worm bred in the hot countries, which grows to many yards' length between the skin and the flesh.*"

"Use a razor," said the oldest, "to chop a flesh-flap, then pull the worm out."

"I would use a snake-charming flute," said the youngest, "and play it near my body and the worm would hear and crawl out the way it came in."

"Down your throat," whispered the middle.

GECK WOULD BE on the flowered couch at his parents' house, where the world sank away. He had stretched across this couch for a lot of years with the same view (brown wall, green chair, white mantel) and in the same sausage-casing, though at different poundages and states of personal hygiene. Today he would be unshaven and thinnish. Wouldn't be thinnish for long unless he started using again. Already he could feel new fat filling the pockety skin. His mother had been cooking up a storm. "Glad to have you home again, honey!" but she was not really that glad about it, nor, God knows, was his father. They were old. They didn't need to be cooking for some son. *He* should have been cooking for *them*, or hiring someone to; he should have been buying them a house in a neighborhood with better trees.

She brought him a blanket and nodded at the television. "Anything fun on?"

"No, Ma."

His leg would feel terrible—throbbing, raw. The old injury made itself known when it was damp out, or when

Geck was especially tired. A wee shot of dodge would have hushed the throb; clean, the whole bone ached. He'd rub arnica down his calf. Arnica was for muscles, not bones, but his legmeat hurt too and he liked the tingle of the medicine. Wanting it all over, that warm shiver, he would wipe the ointment on his forehead.

"Ham salad for supper," his mother would say from the doorway. "How does that sound?"

"Good," Geck would mumble, shifting on the cushions, his boxers disagreeably snug. Time to get some new garb for this plumpening bulk. Perhaps he and his dear mother would take a trip to the mall. They'd walk among the teens, all of whom were having more sex than Geck was; and they would browse for husky sizes; and they would eat cinnamon buns on a plastic bench.

And when he walked into the bar, my first thought was that he was looking better these days—not all withered and sweaty. My next thought was that I'd seen it before, the betterness, and did not trust it at all.

"Tonic water with lime," he said. At Mink's raised eyebrow, he added: "I'm on the wagonista."

"Congratulations," she said. "Again."

"Yeah, well…" His eyelids fluttered.

Mink, humming, busied herself with the nozzles.

"It was my birthday rather recently," he remarked.

"Oh yeah? Happy birthday."

"The big eff oh."

If he was forty, Mink couldn't be far behind. The

same horror'd hit her when he had a birthday on tour: I'll be *thirty* soon? she had said to me, in actual wonder. Geck had been mad at us for not getting him a present and made a series of dark comments about our oversight, particularly mine, since by biblical standards I'd known him better than they did.

"Did I put enough lime in?" asked Mink.

"Yeah," said Geck, "it tastes all right, *considering.*"

She could see he wasn't long for that wagon.

"Anyway, we're playing next Saturday—you should come."

"Sure, uh huh!" she said.

Geck turned to greet his drummer, a battered old guy who still managed to hit the tinies, bequeathing venereal disease to the next generation. I leaned on the faux zinc, under the chandelier, next to an ex–danseur exotique, a dirty-deeds bore who had done all her living already and now roamed the earth putting others to sleep with it.

"Ever had your ass eaten by two guys at once?"

"Why no," I said.

"It's not a laughing matter," she muttered.

I edged away toward glingles-groined Lad, who was complaining: "Why do *I* always have to call?"

"Because you are more charming," Geck said. "Did you talk to that Providence guy? We need to book some additional shit in the north. Hey Minkum, where else did we play in New England?"

I watched her blink. Did she ever miss it, our old life? Being gone for weeks and months on end and how we draped ourselves like characters from a pageant and etched our eyes into flowers, and could have robot-mouths when we wanted, and moved through the world—so it sometimes felt—like a different species entirely? A species akin to, though not the same as, today's genus of the arrow-haired and the fly-eyed?

"Western Massachusetts," she said. "And Maine."

"Oh hell yeah, that VFW where all those earthlings got face-knifed by balders? That was Maine."

"So I'll let you know," said Lad, rising from his stool.

"Yeah, yeah." Geck waved him away and announced to me, "I saw Jupiter and those guys last night. I was on the list or I wouldn't have gone, of course, but anyway, they did a cover of 'Dear Done For.'"

"What'd he say before the song?"

"Oh, just that they were going to play a local golden oldie and hoped we would enjoy it."

"Golden oldie? Those douches are our age."

"That's not what it means," Mink said. "It's more like, the song is a classic. They were doing an homage."

"Mother," I said, "fucks."

I wanted to tell Mink and Geck about the mistake made by the pretty little singer, and hear them scoff at it, and let them convince me it could not have been Cam he saw—that Cam lived in California, in Brazil, in the *Alps* for god's sake and was certainly not riding any subways around here. But I kept thinking about that old sorcery rule about saying people's names out loud. How it brought them back.

MY FATHER WAS digging in the flowers. My sister was cutting with the little scissors. My brother, too young to be trusted, was indoors.

"Fod, come here."

It looked like a stepped-on pomegranate, pink nubs tangled in a smashed fuzz. One nub had rolled away—I went closer—a big seed? With a stick, I prodded it. It had two tiny hands, or starts of hands, stuck together like praying, and a bulby head, and the curl of where legs would grow. It lay in a sack of skin.

"Fod, come *here*."

"Hold your horseradish." He kept digging.

"I can't because there's babies."

"What kind?" asked my sister in her red coat.

"Pink," I said in my blue.

They followed me to the road.

"Mices!" screamed my sister.

"Moles," corrected Fod.

"How did they get on the road?"

"A pterodactyl," she guessed.

"An owl," said Fod. "It must have dropped the mother's body while it was flying, or thrown it up out of its stomach."

"But the babies are alive."

"No, love, they weren't even babies yet—they were still developing."

"But they *are* babies," she insisted.

"No—"

"Yes they are," I chimed.

"No, girls, they're not."

I liked when my parents said *girls* because it made me as much of a girl as my sister, who was more girl. Girls, if this happens one more time, I am not buying cherry juice ever again!—our mother standing furious over a carpet stain; I had knocked over my cup.

My sister at dinner explained about the moles. She didn't tell about the baby she was keeping in a matchbox. It was velvet and rubbery, like an eraser. It was sleeping. Then it went gray. Had she forgotten to leave the box open at night for air to get in? She held a backyard burial to which my brother and I were invited. Flapping her hand over the matchbox she said, "The ground gets you now."

THE ANIMAL'S NAILS were longer than its teeth, body thumping sheetrock as it ran. Could it see me? Where were its holes? It left the wall at night, putting bites in the newspaper and tracks on the counter. I intended to kill it with a hammer. Its nails came through the wall. My brother's breathing used to come through the wall at Observatory Place, thinner plaster than at Edinburgh Lane; his sniffles and coughs had blown into my room where I lay all summer thinking about how Riley had just graduated from a good college whereas I had never even finished my bad one. He had a diploma (he framed it) and I had magazine clippings in a box. During the few hot months before Riley got his own apartment, we talked hardly ever, except to fight over TV channels or the last of the sugar cereal; but when I threw an un-opened beer bottle into the living-room window, he told our parents a bird had flown at the glass.

If only Octy would do battle with the rat, curl a furry tentacle round the vermin neck and wring until death throes, like tiny throat-clearings, could be heard. *But I am too old to fight rats!* Gnashy noises; the rat was chewing—what, a ball of blood and skin? Maybe when the old white lady down the block died the rat would whiff her corpse and find her through the pipes, nibble at the dry sinews, choke on the gristle. When you got that old, did your pubic hair fall out?

The phone rang, and my mother was interested to find out when I'd be settling up a small loan I had promised to pay back by Christmas.

"No, Mert, I know—"

"But you said you—"

"I'll take care of it."

" . . . "

"What's that?" I said.

"I *said*, when do you plan to take care of it?"

"Soon."

"We can't keep lending you money. It's humiliating for you."

I dug my nail bed for a wisp of skin to work at.

"If you can't—"

"Look, as I have already *informed* you, Ajax asked if I minded not getting paid for a couple of weeks because the store is . . . we're having cash-flow challenges. I said fine."

"But why would you—"

"He's my *friend*. And I'm the assistant manager."

In a softer voice: "I'm just worried about you, pettle. It doesn't seem like much of a life."

Red flared in my stomach. I peeled my finger with great care: one strip, two. "I'll write you a check next week," I said.

Octy preferred the couch arm, but was willing to be moved: kitchen counter while I heated up a dinner, bed pillow when I did not want to be in bed alone. The little face of thread mouth and marble eyes could always see me. Its gaze never withered. Good night, I told him, patting a grubby tentacle. Only six were intact—the seventh hacked off by my sister, the eighth gnawed to stub by the pet rabbit of a dirt-child who had lived for a few minutes at the house I rented with Cam and a rotating cast of others on Belfry Street. *Sleep well. You too.* And now the dark bag of room tightening round my body, pressing the quiet at my skull to enlarge the sounds inside. The ring, the ring, *I hated it* and nowhere for it to go, trapped forever in the ears. I once knew a guy who was able to tell what notes his ears were making: C sharp, middle E. *Make sure to wear your earplugs!* They'd bought me fancy ones the Christmas after Cam and I started the band: Promise to wear them? said fiddly old Mert, who hadn't known you couldn't hear your own voice very well with plugs in.

I tapped on the radio, lit a cigarette. Dark whales rode the walls and the fist-fat rat gurgled through the plaster as it dreamed. Mert used to sing us to sleep with "Clementine." A clementine was a baby orange. A rat was a baby devil. Under the radio, impervious to smoke, snarlings of tinsel plinked and bounced. I hit my ear with a palm and slid a game into the machine. Skatepark in the California sun. You chose your own look: silver vest or black glimmie—leather briefs or green pegtops— shaved skull or blond mop. I liked playing as a boy. You could turn the blood function on or off. I kept it on to see his mangled knees and leaking face, gushy spats on the concrete.

"**YOU ARE CADMUS** and I am Europa. We are the kids of a king. The god Zeus stole me to Greece and you looked and looked but couldn't find me. On your search you got advice from an oracle, met a cow, and killed a dragon."

"So can I cut open Dragony's stomach?" I asked, pointing at her stuffed monster.

"No that's *over*, you already killed it and now you are even more sad because you still can't find me."

"This is stupid."

"No Cadmus, it's not stupid, you are sad."

"Can I take a prisoner?" I said. Riley was somewhere downstairs; I could rope his wrists together, pull off his underwear.

"No Cadmus, you are gentle and good."

"Well what am I supposed to *do* then?" I stood in her room wishing we had video games like regular families, or a TV at least. Lack of TV stuck you in rooms with lame sisters who wrapped themselves in sheets, pirouetting, singing "Where am I? Where am I? Where am I?"

When we played Nakedies, my sister would hold a lit lighter to the inside of Riley's fat pink thigh. I'd blindfold him with his superhero undies, the knot so screwy he couldn't undo it himself and so tight he couldn't rip it off, and we'd leave him like that. The weird thing was he never told. I undid the blindfold and whispered, "I bet you will *this* time!" but Riley stared back and said he wouldn't. Why not? "Because I won't," he said. The tears made his eyes so green.

I WOKE IN the night to cramps, the first swelling roll. The pain was veiny brown—a side of killed meat. When I stood, the collecting blood squirted out and I would have to throw these panties away. A girl's stomach was raining. "Why does it look like rain?" my sister had asked, and I crumpled the paper I was using to explain periods to her: "That's just how I drew it." "How do you make the stomachache stop?" "Aspirin," I said.

I thumbed off the cap, shook five into my palm.

In the morning, still bleeding hard, I hobbled to the convenience store, where a boy no older than twelve was buying cigarettes. Two Thumbs was staring at the ceiling. The short aisles contained nothing but plasticked pies. I consulted the soda case. *Will you get me some ginger ale?* Reached for a green bottle. *I have a—* My sister hadn't known yet to call them cramps; she said stomachache. Puddle on the bedsheet: a perfect red sun. Two Thumbs watched the sun through the ceiling; he was refusing to actually be here. I smiled at him and he smiled back but only with the front of his mouth. "Dollar fifteen," he said.

AMONG US THREE, I was boyest. My sister with her painted nails and whimsies was very girl, and Riley, dazed and scuttling, seemed despite his penis not boy at all. I was only half girl, so lanky and teatless, never scenic from across a room.

My sister did her sanding on the sunporch so the flakes of skin wouldn't fall on anything Mert could yell at her for. The porch floor was already a mess. Riley sat at her feet, watching her scrub.

"*Pourquoi* are you doing that?" I asked, swinging past.

"I am making my touch receptors closer to the surface," my sister said. "To sense the teeny grooves of locks, safecrackers' fingers have to be incredibly alert, so they sandpaper off the top layer of skin, which is dead and blocks feeling."

And she held up her hands, dribletting red, ten little pads torn open.

We played on our parents' bed, leaping and twirling in bare skin. Fod came in to tell us time for dinner, and in the middle of the word *dinner* he stopped, muttered "Goddammit," hauled me by the arm away from the little ones and into the bathroom.

He pointed to my downstairs.

Three hairs.

"No more Nakedies for you, hear me?"

THOUGH I HAD been eating again for years and years, the extra hair on my lip and chin had never quite gone away. Your mustache, Riley used to cackle, your beard! I uncapped the jar of cream, the plastic powder vial, scooped portions onto a plastic square and stirred with a tiny paddle. Daubed mixture above mouth and along jawline. Fifteen minutes. I proned myself on the couch so the drying bleach wouldn't fall off. Ten minutes. The bearded lady. The good doctor had explained it was my body's way of staying warm when it couldn't be sure there would be enough flesh to do the job. Five minutes. My arms were still hairy too: I kept them in sleeves. One minute. Hot water and washcloth.

I remembered of course where the notebook was—in my blue cardboard suitcase, stuffed up on the top closet shelf, where I stowed things I couldn't stand to throw away. The notebook was rubber-banded to a cigar box of fan mail. I sat straight down on the floor and opened to an early page.

*Hicky kidlet in blue lipstick whispers, "When
I heard that song Floors it was like you eaves-
dropped my brain." The sparklers are tiny in
Iowa. Child-shaped. The second we started to
play they lined up all dutiful and solemn but
the whole time hardly moved.*

Teased up the page corner to see what might be next—
saw the word *fumes*—then threw it down. But picked it
up again.

*Escape me from these people!!! I have 5 more
weeks with them which I don't know how I
am going to stand. Shows haven't even been
good so far so what is the point? I am hiding in
way back after yelling at M for doing nails in
van (fumes) and I made a crack about vanity
but not even harsh and she starts to actually
C-R-Y and C goes Apologize! and I said Is this
a charm school?*

Smoke rolled off my thin black letters, the colors churned up. Cam had liked to criticize my manners, much like a persnickety aunt. A very tall aunt.

I knelt on the floor and stretched out. *Here I am. Here I am.* The kitchen clock clicked. The rain pelted. The cathedral sat on its hill. *Here I am.* I could hear the colors still, all those terrible bright shapes, but they were knotting together—slowing. I was in my apartment on a street in a city in a country on the floating scab of a globe.

"IF FOD KILLED Riley from punching him in the stomach, what should be his punishment?"

The youngest looked at the oldest, and the oldest looked surprised.

"Come on, what?"

"I don't know," said the oldest.

"There would have to be punishment," said the middle matter-of-factly. "Which do you think: water torture on a schedule, or life imprison?"

ACROSS THE BUS aisle, a calamity-haired baby spark had been sneaking glances. It was a half recognition—he couldn't quite place me. Hope crackled. *Hey I fucking loved your last record* was what they usually said. Then hope dashed on the rocks of shame: had I fallen so low I needed a high-school student to remember my name? I put my cheek to the window glass and snapped the band, wanting pain so bright it was all I felt.

The familiar room of crimson walls, black floor. Geck nursed a tonic water in a booth. If battling to stay off mood alterers, I didn't know why one would want to hang out where they were sold; but this was his pattern. Every time he got clean he persisted in moping around the bar, sighing a lot, twirling a dirty pale forelock on his finger.

"Watch any good moving pictures lately?" he wanly inquired.

"Last night I saw a decent one about life on a planet run by people who look like whippets."

"What the fuck is a whippet."

"You know, like a very thin dog."

He tipped back the glass. Ice cubes kicked against his teeth. "I have a cane," he announced, "made from the penis of a bull."

"Is that right."

"Serious," he nodded. "Buddy of mine from treatment got it for me, on account of my leg. Minky!" he shouted. "Can I have another of these? With olives this time?" He added to me: "Imperative to give yourself some variety."

Geck had fifty-two days. Eight more until sixty, then thirty to ninety. When he hit ninety he'd be feeling much better. It was always the way. When he felt better, or better enough, he'd start to itch again. He had, as usual, a fat list of complaints about the recovering life. First of all, everyone was always so bleeding grateful. *My name is Bucky and I'm grateful to be sober one more day; my name is Lucky and I have a hell of a lot of gratitude this evening; my name is Sucky and I'm just honored to be alive!* Earlier this evening Geck had eaten five powdered doughnuts from the church table and had not been grateful. Some nights the meetings were a comfort, offering the solace of being among barely-making-it people who, like himself, survived each day on routines of coffee, cigarettes, and self-deprecation; but tonight no solace, merely a bad mood made worse by doughnut-nausea. And Deep Cleavage flirting with the asshole who lied about his clean date. And that dragons 'n swords nidget in his cape.

And bus riding in suburbia—the fucking worst! Took an hour to go a mile, and the other passengers were these huddly little no-life-having people who reminded you, kind of, of yourself. He missed his hatchback. Hated asking for rides so suffered the bus and the endless walk after.

"Such as, for instance, tonight," he concluded, "it'll take me a year to get home. Unless maybe I could crash at your…?"

"Nein," I said. "So is there anyone nice at your meetings?"

"Nice? Um… developmentally *disabled*, maybe. Boring, absolutely. This one guy won't shut up about how his coworker keeps putting his stapler on the guy's side of their workstation…"

And his parents' house was always quiet, I imagined: carpets on every floor, footfalls hidden, a soft agitation snaking down every hall.

"Jonathan? Can I get you a soda?" Geck's mother pronounced *soda* like it was God's greatest temptation. About twenty times a day she offered him one. The ice-box was crammed with six-packs of the various colas, the lemon-limes.

"No thanks," he shouted.

"You sure, hon? I can bring it up."

He licked and flipped slithery pages. His mother had had magazines waiting when he got out of Canterbury Recovery Center, a neat pile on his desk. Well, *their* desk. Everything was theirs. He had paid for nothing in this house except his guitar and a practice amp the size of a keychain.

He told me now, "I guess it's a taxi for me, then. An expensive and unnecessary fucking taxi."

"By the way," I said, "have you seen anyone around lately? Anyone who isn't usually around?"

"You speak in riddles." He dug around in his nose with one pinky, almost delicately.

"Just, I don't know, the other day on the train I thought I saw someone who used to live here—from back in the day—"

"Well, *I* haven't, and I'm glad. I don't need any run-ins with former associates until I've improved my circumstances."

REPORTER LAST NIGHT said how does it feel to be the inspiration for hundreds of fledgling operations? and I felt kind of good because guy is from prominent national magazine that hears of every trend ten years after the fact—and I say humbly, Every new band that starts is good news, and he writes that down, and C snickers from the other side of the room which I could kill him for because you get over here and do the fucking interview then! but he's just sitting there twisting key on snare—and reporter goes, So do you have any advice for those who are just starting out? and I say merrily Don't get a day job! (wow what a brilliant imagination you have Quinn) but the question makes me think about how old I am, a quarter century, and how starting-out kids are so young, like me and C summer after h.s. with all our hopes. I don't want to be just OK, C said that first

summer, I want to be good. We'll be genius,
I promised, secretly concerned I wouldn't be
able to sing and play at the same time, which
proved to be a well-founded worry but who
cares now that we've got Geck whose guitar
charms the snakes from their holes?

THE AMP HAD been banished to the hour between five and six and absolutely zero after dinner because the racket made Mert want to cut off her ears. I tried to play along with songs I liked but couldn't and it sounded like a field of circles with tiny black dots.

"Green-legged triangles!" countered my sister. "Not circles. *Listen.*"

I still heard circles, which infuriated her. "You're not listening close enough. *That*"—when I clanged out a chord—"is *triangle.*"

"It's circles. I'm the musical one, I should know."

"You're actually really bad," she told me.

"Shut up."

"I'm just making a scientific appraisal," she said, "of the facts. Your ability to play is nonexistent."

"Shut *up*," I yelled.

Riley, flower on wall, waited in excitement.

She went on: "I hope you learn soon because otherwise Fod will think it was a big goddamn waste of money."

"I'll do you a mischief," I warned.

"Oh I'm *so scared!*"

I stood up. "You want to get smashed?"

"Nay," said my sister, and there it ended, disappointing our brother, who loved to watch us hit.

The blindfold made loud blackness, a hiss and reel across the backs of his eyes. He was afraid to touch the walls—their surfaces, when bumped, were damp and moving—and his own whines had a horrible pulse. The blackness lasted so long he had stopped crying and was nearly asleep by the time our father opened the closet door and said, "Goddammit" and yanked off the blindfold.

Riley saw the heat in Fod's face. His sisters were going to get hit. He cried, "No Fod, it was a game!"

"A game?" shrugged our father, thundering downstairs.

Riley rushed behind: "Yes and I knew I would be in the closet so it's not bad and I just fell asleep before it was over. Please don't do anything to them."

"Quinn!" Fod shouted at the door to the basement. "Get your ass up here!"

"No Fod *don't*, they didn't *do* anything."

"Look, I'm not about to let them think it's acceptable to leave you tied up in a closet."

"But I wanted them to," Riley shrieked. When he heard our reluctant feet on the stairs, he began to cry again.

THE RING WAS louder than usual, a stinging drone, shiny larvae trapped in the canals try to scream their way out. The only way to halt the ring was sleep. Please fall. Please fall. I smoked in the dark, ashtray cold on bare belly, picturing a hard green cliff soundless but for the wash of the sea. Please, please fall. *So will you switch places now? Okay, but only this one time.*

But it was not naptime; it was family-dinner time.

Put your boots on, Quinn.

They waited dutifully next to a red chip can on the kitchen floor. But my socks were too big, or the leather had shrunk. Shove, shove. Fuck. Wait—*there.* Yes. Now the laces. I wrapped one around my finger, tighter, tightest, the fingertip bursting. A gorged red nub. If all the blood stayed in the finger, it couldn't run down the thigh.

The last frost was over, and my father was busy planting. In non-football months, his passion was the garden. He squatted on the gray dirt, looking thickened, old. I did not want him ever to die.

I would eat for my mother's sake three bites of bread, nine bites of potato, and no bites of baby sheep. Couldn't let her know I was counting again, that the worm was here again, or that all the wisdom I'd gotten from the good doctor felt iced over like a museum sword. The worm, which had been gone for years and years, was sniffing again. Looking for blood. And why? The sudden hot fear of Cam being back? But he wasn't even back. Some little pinstripe had just seen his double.

I dried my hands on the reindeer towel.

Mert called, "I'm doing asparagus. You like that, don't you?"

"I…"

"Quinn?"

"Yeah."

Twelve bites, but small.

We were not religious, had never gone to church except for funerals, but on this Easter Sunday our mother had seen fit to roast a lamb and unscrew a jar of mint jelly.

"*My*, this is Christian!" bellowed daughter. Silence. She tried again: "What did the moneylender say to Jesus?"

Son smiled.

The platters of food to bring out.

"I can help," Riley said, rising to follow. "You could help too," he called over his shoulder at me. "…"

"What's that?"

"*Beverages.*"

"Okay, well, what does everybody want?" I asked without getting up.

Fod said, "I haven't had lamb in God knows how long. Have you?"

"I'm a no-flesher," I reminded him.

"Still? Well, good for you…"

I dipped a finger in the jelly jar, licked it.

"That's pretty disgusting," he said.

My mother brought a plate of bright stalks. Our pee was going to smell.

Dark on my underwear—the fifteen-year-old Quinn had hoped it was from asparagus. Please be the asparagus. No, it was blood. At first it made no more than brown breath on the cotton, but by morning it was falling red and real. Oh no oh no oh no.

"Mert forgot napkins," explained Riley, throwing them at me and Fod, who wasn't looking—his hit him in the face.

"Jesus," he said mildly.

In the day, there would have been consequences. A slam of the table and a raised voice; or, before my sister died, a slap. Time had diluted all of Fod's intensities. He still loved football, but not in that maniac way. Every autumn Sunday of our childhood he had been at the bar or next door at the Walkers'. If the team lost, family dinner could be expected to be awful. I don't understand, Mert would say, what's so fascinating about men jumping on top of one another; and Fod always answered, Then I feel sorry for you.

It was a sore subject too because I'd never liked football and had resisted my father's early attempts to school me in it. Come watch with me! Mrs. Walker has the good kind of chips— No thanks, Fod. Oh, it'll be fun, I'll explain everything—it can be a little confusing at first—No, Fod. I was a bad child, I knew; other children were not bored by football, and could enjoy it with their fathers, could impress their fathers with memorized statistics and game analysis.

When I tried to swallow, the wedged potato resisted. One mouthful of water forced it down the esophagus, another into my stomach.

Mert was watching with the old worry, from the bad times. "Are you feeling sick?"

I nodded and tapped my forehead.

"Well, at least try some more potato."

I goaded a small bite onto my fork. Two more made three. Six more made nine. If I only ate nine, the worm couldn't come. *Worm you are banished.* Stop and breathe, the good doctor had said. When you start counting or listing, fill your lungs with air. But if I breathed, I would eat, and if I ate, the blood-logged worm would come sniffing.

Mert clamped a hand on my elbow.

"Sorry," I said, "what?"

"Back to Earth, pettle! I said do you want pistachio or chocolate?"

"Neither."

"Oh, but it's the brand you like, just have a little bit—"

"No *thank* you, Mert."

"So kids," Fod cut in, "have you been reading about the torture in the army prisons?"

Mert said, "Let's not talk about the war, please."

"But the war is happening."

"So is dessert, and we don't need to discuss torture while we eat."

"Yeah, well, we're fortunate to have the luxury of—"

"Stop it," she said.

"But—"

"I *said*—"

I scratched my wrist, hard, while my brother built a sculpture of lamb bone and jelly.

"NO IT IS *not* yellow, it's silverish and a girl. *Eight* is yellow."

"Eight is yellow?"

"Of *course*, Fod."

He shrugged. "My eight's red."

"Mine too," my sister said and I was alone; then she reminded me, "But our sevens are both purple and boys!" and I was not alone.

"This conversation is boring for some of us," said Mert, whose numbers did not have colors.

"Is your nine green?" continued Fod.

"Yes," I said happily. "Also three is green a little, but mixed with blue."

"Hmm, my three is orange," he said.

"No, black!" my sister shouted.

"How can three be *black*?"

"It just is," she said.

But only a zero could be black, not any of the regular numbers. They were talking about something else now, but my head kept pounding on the fact of the black three.

"Remember you've got the—"

Triplet prongs dripped with melted night: a gruesome, furious three.

"Back to Earth, Quinn!"

I turned glazily to my mother: "What?"

"I said I'll pick you up at two thirty tomorrow."

"Why?"

"The *dentist.* So all those aspiring cavities can get their due."

I BROUGHT THE cigar box to work to rake through my trove, the yellowed sheaf of old mail—too embarrassed, of course, to read it when anyone was around, so I waited to pull the box from my bag until Ajax had gone out. "Defend the compound," he instructed as usual, and saluted.

> Thank you for making such incredible music, it is really getting me through, when I am in a bad state I put you on and it makes the shadow leave and I want to say thanks.
>
> Yrs forever,
>
> Dagger
> Cleveland, Ohio

Ah, Dagger, dear stripling. Ours forever. I rubbed my wrist. And the Neptune Beach letter, another favorite:

Hi kids!!! Down in the ditch of pathos and
ennui that is upper Florida, we celebrated
your new record by throwing a Suicide Party.
Guests were required to announce at the door
their preferred method of self-offing. We are
one thousand strong, your swamp fans.

You stood on a stage and people loved you. You yelled
for thirty minutes and they knew the words better than
you did. You drank for free beforehand, and during, and
after. Liquor was plied; necks were slavered upon. The
crappy sadness of a sports bar in a midwestern city on
a Tuesday could be concealed, even changed by the sla-
vering and plying. We had met with luck in the hospi-
tality department. Local outcasts, who relied on music
for their reason to wake, welcomed us to their hamlets
in the manner of younger cousins at a family reunion,
escorting the more august relatives to the best lawn
chairs, bringing them extra helpings of slaw. Eat with us
tonight? Drink with us tonight? Sleep with us tonight?

Nobody had come through the door in two hours.
I'd counted the ceiling tiles many times but began again,
certain not to be interrupted. The string of bells on the
door clinked softly in a push of wind; an ambulance
shrieked from Wisconsin Avenue; I counted and counted and lost my place and had to start over. A beef patty
abandoned by Ajax had drawn a spider, who made a me-
thodical journey across the cold meat. We're in trouble,
Ajax had told me the day before. Revenue was taking

a serious dive. But revenue had been taking dives for such a long while that I couldn't bring myself to be concerned; the store would prevail, as it always had, in the face of corporate cupidity and the Web. The city's loyal sparks and mock intellectuals, along with isolates who liked to mail order, would keep us clinging to life.

At the clinkle of bell string I glanced up, ready to chuck a hollow How's it going? at whoever had wandered in at day's end; but it was, to my surprise, my brother. Behind him stood a long, milk-colored girl.

"This is Pine," rushed Riley, "and this is Quinn…"

I shoved the mail into its box, dropped the box under the counter. The girl shook my hand with a papery palm: "Pleased to meet you." She had a husky little British accent.

Riley added, "We just stopped by to say hello."

He never stopped by. Was this his *lady friend*? Or was she merely a fellow picture-filer at the archives who liked to sit quietly among dead people's faces? She was so pasty you could see the veins in soft blue strings down her arms. Her garb—khakis and accountant vest—was even more gruesome than my brother's. They hunched daily in the same bunker. Once in a while Riley must have come across a weird one, an interesting one; these maybe he showed to Pine before filing; but the archive photos on the whole were unremarkable documents to be sorted and stored and never looked at again. The chief, catching them bent over a streaked shot of two women in wheelchairs holding either end of a banner—*Mr.*

President how long must women wait for liberty?—hurried to scold: You are paid to be meticulous, not to frolic. He put a warning hand on Riley's shoulder. Pine stared at the hand. Riley stared at the photo—*Suffrage march, 1917*—until the fingers went away.

"Hello," I said.

"Nice shop," Pine said.

"Quinn doesn't own it," Riley was quick to assure her. "Just an employee."

"Assistant manager," I said.

FOD EVENTUALLY STOPPED asking if I wanted to go next door to the Walkers' for the game. I figured he was waiting for Riley to be old enough to appreciate football. It was hard, even then, to imagine Riley appreciating football.

One day my sister said, "I'll go."

Fod, shocked: "You really want to watch the game?"

"Sure, why not," she said. She was already getting into her coat.

And she smelled like trees.

And she loved Cadmus and Europa, would bribe me to play it: a marble, a dollar, some chocolate. I waited while she tore a sheet from the bed to wrap herself in.

"Oh Cadmus, what shall become of me?"

"Who cares," I said.

"No," my sister whispered, "you have to say: *You are lost and gone forever, dreadful sorry, Europa mine!*"

I repeated the sentence without enthusiasm.

"Again," she ordered. "Say it again."

"WAS THAT YOUR girlfriend?"

"Shut up."

"Was it?"

"Shut up."

"What are you, *twelve?*—was that, or was that not, your girlfriend who came with you to the bookstore?"

"No it was not," Riley said.

"Okay then."

"Why do you ask?"

"*Out of curiosity.*"

"Did . . . ?"

"What's that?"

"Did we look like a couple?" he hollered.

"Not especially, no."

The eggs on my plate were blisters of pus and my throat was shutting, but I managed a few mouthfuls so Riley wouldn't notice. A bullet was a mouthful of pennies. My brother was done with his oatmeal. The waitress refilled our coffees. I watched him pour white blood into the cup.

"She grew up in a remote village," he said.

"Who?"

"My *friend*. Pine. She's kind of different because of being English but also from a village."

"Hmm."

"And she wants you to come for dinner."

"Me?"

"Us. She invited us. She likes to cook."

"But I don't know her," I said.

"She's my friend. Please?"

Remembering what I was about to ask for, I said, "Sure, of course. I'll check my schedule." I straightened up in the booth. "Also. I was wondering something."

Riley narrowed his cute eyes. He knew I was about to beg. It was not hard to guess: I was wearing the fake-nice face. The face bothered him more than the begging.

"The first is coming up," I said, "and I'm a tiny bit short."

"I can lend you some," he said sadly.

"That'd be great. I'll pay you back in a week."

"All right."

"No seriously I will!"

"I believe you," he lied.

CAM ONCE EXPLAINED to my brother that Stradivarius had sprinkled volcanic ash between the wood and the varnish on his violins, lushening their sound. "Well, that's the theory." A smile, a push of black hair back. "Next time I build a guitar," he added, "I might try it."

Unlike most of us, Cam actually knew how to do things.

"But where would you get the volcanic ash?" asked Riley.

"I know a few ash dealers," Cam said.

"Now get out," I told Riley, who was knifing slivers he didn't plan to eat from a hunk of cheese.

"It's not your kitchen," he whimpered. "It's Mert and Fod's kitchen."

"Get the fuck *out* of here!"

"Don't be an asshole," Cam told me.

FROM THE SUBWAY I climbed to a street ateem with suited normals and walking-homers and, here and there, an aimless spark lighting the first smoke of nightfall. I passed a crone hauling a one-eyed dog under her arm. Where the second eye should have been was a pucker of fur and skin. This stupid city, why did I love it? Its buildings were mostly not beautiful; its couture was often terrible; and many parts of town were as segregated as they had been in the fifties. But I'd been a baby here; my childish lungfuls had been of this air; and here I had become some mock version of adult. I creaked like one, had the scuffed look of one; but indoors, I was not much better than fifteen.

Uphill past the park, toward the churches, I winced at the streak on my lungs. Creak, creak. I used to make this walk no problem, sucking cigarettes.

I tripped and slammed my head into a lamppost. Forehead wet, fingers red. How much beer was at home? There'd better be enough, and the game-machine had better not stall again tonight or I would kill it. "Kill," I said aloud, wiping my hand on my britches. In case I was out at home, it might be safer to go directly to the bar.

DON'T BE SCARED, said my sister. Don't. Because it's not scary, it's *good*! Some famous people have it. Like the Russian writer—and the French composer—it's a *talent*. Don't you want to be talented? Yes you do. You can't be scared. Fod's not, is he? and *I'm* not, so you don't have to be. You know how sometimes you wish you could rip everything out of your head? Like there is too much noise in it? Well, this is what I do: lie on your back like this—*watch*, Quinn—and close your eyes and say, Here I am. Here I am. Here I am.

PINE ANNOUNCED, "WE are going Moroccan tonight!"

Riley unlaced his rain-drippy shoes and left them by the door. I did the same. The girl must have been particular about floors.

I sniffed: "Chicken?"

"North African recipe," Pine nodded.

"Um, okay."

Riley widened his eyes at me.

I mouthed, *What?*

He asked Pine chipperly, "So when are you going to tell me your real first name?"

She snorted. "You wouldn't want to know, I *assure* you. It's a very hideous name."

"Then how come your parents—"

But she ran into the kitchen. Riley and I sat dumbly until she returned with steaming plates and cried, "Chicken *magnifique*! Just let me get the bread…"

I inspected the meat. What were those dots? Wrinkled brown—*fuck*. The sky went thick rust-purple with the smoke of scalded grape: fizzling, flattening, blackening dots on their pyre. All gone. All gone.

"What's wrong?" Pine called from the kitchen.

"Nothing," said Riley.

"But somebody made a weird sound." She came back in, wiping fingers on a dishtowel. "Is it undercooked?"

"No," I said, "I just can't—"

"You don't like the sauce?"

"No—no—it's the—" The sky was so heavy, so fucked-ly purple, I almost gagged. Every atom of killed raisin hit my lung hairs. My mother shook me by the shoulders.

Riley held a glass to my mouth. I sipped. "Sorry."

"No, no," said Pine, "you're *ill*, don't apologize."

"I'm allergic to raisins."

Pine smiled. "Violently, it would seem."

Red boxes in single file on the sill, lined up along the baseboard, stacked in a pyramid on my desk. The guidance counselor in his bolero tie had repeated, "Bonfire?"

"It wasn't a bonfire," I insisted.

"All right," said Mert, "*blaze*. Conflagration. Inferno."

I'd hoped the counselor was noticing my mother's tendency to exaggerate. *I refuse to cook food night after night for people who do not appreciate it.* I hoped he would write it down in a file.

"And there was nothing else being burned except—?"

"That's right," said Mert, "which is what concerns me most. It feels like a ritual, some kind of cult thing."

"Why raisins?" the counselor asked. I shrugged. The counselor waited, asked again.

"There were some lying around," I said.

"Fifty-five boxes!" screamed Mert. "Those little snack size! I counted—"

"You went into my *room*?"

My mother had been wrong: there were not fifty-five boxes—that was not a good number at all—there were fifty-seven. But I did not correct her. The guidance counselor asked again, "Why raisins?" and I smelled the sky, swollen rust-purple with the smoke of their dying.

"Do you need to go home?" said Pine now.

"No!" Riley said.

"Maybe," I said, holding a hand over my lips so the worm couldn't get out.

THE WILD WEST game was boring: you rode a bull around a ranch to save a girl. Always a girl. God forbid a *fellow* should ever find himself in need of saving. I chopped down the short list of distractions—more beer, another game, auto-pleasuring. Or walking (hood up, eyes down) whither and nither round the night city, blinked at by cats. I was homesick for teendom, when everything had stretched like a road. I'd decided to be a singer so I could lure Cam's best friend, the hot Pete, from a girlfriend who did not sing. I'd planned to make up for my average physiognomy by being the pivot. The engine. I would make them look. I would do weirdness with my voice that wasn't pleasing or pretty but made them look. My melodies (what passed for them) were blue or silver or bruise. Like runny fabric they bled on my eyes—not my eyeballs but the ones behind them, the louder eyes I'd wished my whole life I could turn off.

Did Pete ever hear *Purgastoria*, or any of the earliers? By the time our first record came out he was gone. When we played near his college, some meadowy town in New England, he was in the audience. He saw me see him—nodded—but left before our set was over. I did not tell Cam.

In the table drawer I kept a book borrowed years ago from the library: *Enchantments of the Octopus.* I opened to a middle page:

> Strange mating ritual of argonaut octopus in Mediterranean   female waits while some distance away male accumulates se-men in ventral cavity   extracts semen with a tentacle   tentacle separates from male's body, floats toward female, enters her belly, lets loose semen into her organs   arm is messenger bringing male's hoard to female male knows nothing of the beauty he's hacked off a limb for and female knows of her mate only the fertilizing arm.

One Christmas in midchildhood I'd gone downstairs with my sister very early and in the dark we stared at the stockings. She tried to guess the gifts from the bulges. Tree smell prickled the walls of my nose. Under the cold was black from dead candles. I'm going to look for just one tiny second, I explained, and was hauling a chair to the mantelpiece when Fod (where had he snuck from?) said "Greedy!" and I stopped, red. But the shame faded fast, replaced by excitement at my presents, the octopus most. It was soft and gray with a sewn-on mouth and black marble eyes. Fod said each arm had a different power, and it would be up to me to learn what all the powers were.

Only the fertilizing arm.

The other thing in the drawer was the old bike chain. Greenish-blackish links cold on my skin, Cam on my skin, the chain hard between my chest and his pressed ear. When he'd said *I want to hear,* I let him listen. Mineral neck. Sopping panties slicked up tight to the bone. In Milwaukee, I had wanted him again. *My fingers are ten spots of blood who remember you.*

TODAY HE GOES, *Planning any collect calls to your little shaver? What is a shaver. From the other night the one in 10th grade. He was of age, I said. Of age to what, go down on you before he does his social studies homework? He was 21 actually. If you believe that says C you are even stupider than I thought. I just hope you kept it to oral because otherwise he's got a statutory case against you. Can we change the subject? says M who was driving and therefore had authority since whoever's driving can claim they're going to crash if people don't change the subject. So C shut up and in the roadwatch silence I figured it out. Reason for all his bitchiness yesterday. HE IS JELLLLLUSSSSSS!*

THE PONG OF cheap meat and fry oil hung on the air. Little paper boats rode the counter, too grease-sogged to be ashtrays; I tapped my cigarette into a coffee can. On the wood paneling behind the register was a prehistoric poster from a place downtown that had been converted several years ago into a wine bar: gunpowder silk screen of a witch taking off her spiky hat to reveal a headful of cassettes, and in swooping letters the names of the bands. That had been a good show; I'd gone with Cam, who was acquainting me with the romance of the set list and the hand stamp. The first time I ever bleached my hair, Fod said at the table: So now you're some kind of deviant? I'd expected my mother to be mad too, but she seemed not really to notice. (After my sister died, she noticed everything less.) Riley said, I bet if you put a thing in your nose she won't give a crap either. A *thing*? sneered I. The new hair had made me feel the same way buying records did: like I lived in a secret country. After a trip to the record store, I'd spread out my purchases on the bedroom floor, each to inspect, to adore. I would play the records in a row then play them again, and again. I did not skip the weaker songs, because Cam had taught me you couldn't always tell at first. There was a three-listen rule. If interrupted by school or dinner, I switched off the player but kept the needle on the vinyl exactly where it had halted.

Another flier, older, tacked higher on the paneling: *Show off or shut up!!! $3, all you can hear.*

And now I was someone to whom slender boys felt they could say, Whatever, lady!— unaware that I'd once stood on stages.

Most shameful of all, I cared about this.

Ajax said, "I know we've already been tightening belts, but we have to do something drastic. Last month's revenue was a horror show." Fingering the wooden arrow in his earlobe, he squinted out the front window. "I mean *horror.*"

"Mmm."

"I don't really know what else can be done, barring— well, barring."

Ajax would always be worried about money. He didn't understand that we were a beloved local necessity that would carry on into perpetuity.

He said, "Mind not taking your check again this round?"

"Um, no problem." *Dear Mother and Father: I regret to inform you that I will be moving back home at your earliest convenience.*

"Thanks, man, I really—"

The radio said, "A report released last week describes female interrogators in U.S. prisons in Iraq, Afghanistan, and Guantánamo smearing menstrual blood on Islamic prisoners and taunting them with the threat that they will not be given water to purify themselves before prayer."

A clawed brown cheek, three red stripes, a white hand laughing.

My elbow, daubed with my sister's blood. She'd had her period all over herself.

SHE *BECAME A WOMAN* three months before she died. It was a school day, but she hadn't come down yet. Our mother called and called up the stairs. "Go tell that lazy lass to get a move on," she told me, "it's seven fifteen!"

"I have a stomachache," my sister said. "Will you get me some ginger ale?"

"We don't have ginger ale," I said.

She yawned, kicked the covers off, swung her legs down, and creakily stood. A red puddle lay in the bed.

"It's food for a baby," I explained. "It grows on the walls of this pouch. If you don't have a baby that month, the food falls down and comes out from your downstairs. It looks like blood but isn't exactly."

My sister stared at the picture I was drawing. A girl's stomach was raining. Black droplets fell to her feet. "Every month it falls out for about five days," I added.

"But how do you know when?"

"When what?"

"When it's going to come out, so you can put the pad there."

I shook my head: "No, it's not like that. It's—always."

She was shocked. "The *whole* time?"

"Yeah, but there's a little break in the middle and not as much comes on the later days."

"And does your stomach hurt for the whole time?"

"Not the whole time," I said.

AFTER WORK, WALKING home from the subway, I decided on twenty-four slivers of carrot. Twenty-one bites of spinach. The good doctor had said to stop and breathe when I felt myself making a list. Against the breath, stronger than breath, the list continued: nine bites of hard-boiled egg. Why must everything, the good doctor had asked, be divisible by three?

When butter was cooking, I saw whitish chicken yellow and all my blood swarmed to the temples. Hot butter looked like raw fat in the gash in my sister's head; it smelled like worms in the flesh of gashed girls. A worm was a foot and a stomach. From the stomach came juice that unstitched your flesh. Fizzling butter was the fat that had bled from my sister. Please stop cooking that please stop. Quinn, you can't be this sensitive and expect everyone to cater to it. But can't you use olive oil instead? No, said Mert, the recipe calls for—

When beef was cooking I saw the bloodworm, and stomach juice hurt my throat. I ran up the sidewalk with a hand on my mouth—fleshy grease from the restaurant kitchens—and people were staring, because I was crying. With the other hand I wiped my eyes. If I took the first hand away, all the juice would spill. The bloodworm was gliding out of my sister's eye cavity, its own bulging eyes grown over with a fine membrane—it navigated by odor. The worm made no sound. In and out of holes it went, chasing meat with its nostrils. It pecked flesh with tiny teeth the shape of nails. It had eaten her whole face. It had gorged until its skin was stretched so tight it had to stop; and my sister's body waited for the worm to start eating again. The bloodworm had lain on my sheet in the morning. I'd thrown the sheet and mattress pad and my underwear away. If Fod were to see my underwear— I waited until he'd put out all the trash, then brought my stains secretly to the curb. There was always more for the worm to eat unless you hid every drop.

The soldier doused her gusset with food coloring, walked into the interrogation room, shoved her hand into her pants, and brought up a red palmful. She smeared it on the face of the Muslim detainee, for whom contact with a woman on her period was, according to the U.S. Army's manuals on Arab culture, forbidden. This was more than contact: this was the womb itself in tracks down his cheek.

From bed I watched the walls for a telltale thump or bulge. The walls were naked. My most recent New Year's

resolution had been to blanken. I'd ripped away everything. Silk-screened posters for great shows of old;
black-and-white pictures of my body on stages; album
covers I loved anchored by a nail at each corner. All had
gone to the floor and stayed for days, tripping me in
the night. Then I'd gathered everything up to burn but
didn't know where. Too much smoke for indoors, and
out in the yard might attract a cop and cops scared me.
The fear was unreasonable, especially for somebody as
white as I was in a neighborhood where they expected
black people to do the crimes. I'd just heaped the re-
jectamenta in a corner of the kitchen and thrown newspapers on top.

The pink was darker where a flier or photograph had
been, but the sun would do its work. My throat felt regular. No hands at it. I hadn't been visited by the freakeries
since the band days. They used to come when I was too
neezled to ignore them. In a hot-walled bar somewhere
south, one of those blank medium towns, a whole night
had been full of freakeries, corner of the eye, corner of
the eye. On their wooden stumps they had jumped *just
quick enough* out of my sight line.

> *C still scorns me for the sexual relations with
> G, and I scorn me too every time G says some-
> thing stupid, which is every time the mouth
> opens. But the Offer rests on him. He is the
> reason for it.*

Geck brought us star. He gave us shredding divo, oily yellow hair flying as he flailed and twirred and flung to the whole room's heart's content. He was good enough—idiot-savantly gifted enough—that he could play amazing even when loaded. If he fell off the stage, he never lost his place in the song. If he kicked a boy in front and the boy bit his ankle back, Geck went on picking and grinning.

The scout said, "The guitar parts are *insane!*"

So we tolerated. I tolerated most. I let him in. I hated that Cam knew it. *What kind of conversations do you guys have afterward? Can he even have a conversation?*

MY SISTER WAS extratalented in the odor department. She could smell on a book the reaction of the last person to read it. Crouched on the library carpet, she put her nose to the open Bible page: *The woman was worried about not being good enough.* And a dust-black hardcover: *The man got mad because he didn't understand this.* And a fat paperback with a flame-haired nurse falling into the arms of a soldier: *The girl liked this story better than her life.*

She could smell on a clean knife in the kitchen which flesh it had sawed the day before. This went into a baby sheep leg, she'd say. This made cubes from the chest of a chicken.

Sickening food delighted her. Revolting creatures did not alarm her. The snails on Edinburgh Lane had no houses, were tubes of hard jelly that left smears on the sidewalk, and I couldn't stand their bald, stalked eyes; but she picked them up. "You look like a banana," she said, "and you look like puke." They were not snails, she informed me, they were slugs and they wouldn't hurt me and it was stupid to be worried.

"I'm not," I said.

"Yes you are because you're scared of the colors and noises."

"I just don't want them in my head."

"That's because you're afraid," she reasoned. "If you don't be afraid, then it's not bad if they're there." She cuddled two squirming tubes in her palm.

And fat bled from her head. It was the color of blood but also of fat: whitish yellow. It had brains mixed in. When the medics turned her over, brains and fat in a lace of red globbed onto the pillow. Her brain had many things in it: the length of a giant squid, the way to the library, the story of Lacustrina who lived in a lake and had a silver heart no boy could break.

DATE ON MILK was two months prior. I opened the soft triangle mouth: it had gone penis-cheese. But something about the stink was relaxing, a proof of nature's workings—the reliable progress of decay. While my body collapsed, cell by cell, the milk was dying even faster. The rat, too, would meet its maker long before I did, unless it managed to infect me with twenty-first-century plague. The rat carried, I was certain, all manner of disease into the apartment, dropping flecks from his tiny brown lips; when he chewed newspaper his saliva dried to spores. Scamper, scamper, bump. *I'm going to hammer out your brains.* Are rat brains the same color as human? (When the little rabbit cut its foot on a nail at Belfry Street I'd been shocked that its blood looked just like a person's.)

The day was warmish. I stood naked in the kitchen, sweat nipping between my thighs. When I scratched, my shoulder felt padded—with defrosted burritos and maple doughnuts. The red-eyed doll, the dragon, the sailor sat over notched scars. Before I'd gotten all the work done, the scars had been tiny bottle caps under the skin. Mert had sent me to the dink after she barged in—I'd forgotten to lock the bathroom—and saw. We did not talk about it; Mert simply made an appointment and said she would pick me up from school at two thirty. The dink asked me to roll up my sleeve and I said no and the dink waited, then asked again, and I said no again. Your mother tells me you've been hurting yourself, said the dink.

I brought the candy bar, my old knife, and sandwich bags to the couch and began to slice. Octy counted with me: one, two, three on up to thirty-nine. Each sandwich bag received six slices, which made six bags, and I was allowed to eat the remaining three right away. As I brought the first tiny piece to my mouth, I heard a whistling.

Let me back in!

Whistling turned to howling. Teeth hit the glass.

I ate the second and third pieces and gathered up the bags. "Stop it," I said.

But please.

"Stop it, I can't let you in!" I bumbled toward the kitchen, eyes closed so I wouldn't see my sister.

The whistling quit and I opened my eyes. On the counter, next to a can of cheese, the hammer waited for its chance. Just show your face, I told the rat, and the floor'll be wearing your brains! I was talking out loud again. The first sign. Not of mental illness—those symptoms usually appear by late youth—it was something worse, not glamorous at all. *Crumble-brain.*

MY SISTER MADE her mouth an O and puffed at Riley. "What does it smell like?"

He shrugged. "Your mouth, I guess."

"Is it bad?"

"I don't know."

"Is it like onions?"

"Why, you ate some?"

She blew into her palm and sniffed. "There's this thing called period breath and I want to know if I have it. Some women give off an *oniony smell* during their menstrual. If it happens to me, I'll—"

"Kill yourself?" I suggested from across the room.

"Go to a breath doctor," she said.

Riley leaned to smell again. "It might be a *little* oniony," he admitted.

> This tale is of Lacustrina, who lived in a lake.
> She had the head of a girl and the legs of a
> snake. She had a silver heart no boy could

break. She loved to sleep but preferred to wake. She envied the mermaids their saltwater cake of such elegant sweetness it made your tongue ache.

You are Cadmus. I am Europa. I am stolen. You spent a long time looking, never found. You killed a dragon, and planted his teeth, and soldiers grew from the ground.

MINK'S DAUGHTER WAS cute but clearly an only child, accustomed to being the sole getter of attention. My own ego problems stemmed (was my theory) from those two and a half years before my sister: the newborn me in a basket, oohed and ahhed over; the baby me in her high chair, reveling in hours of gaze; the toddler me, destroying furniture but not getting punished because I was their one and only pettle. Naturally I'd been angry when another showed up. Siblings protected you from spoiling, since there was never quite enough to go around.

After the soup, Mink brought out a plate of macaroons. Meli said she didn't want any.

"What's up, bee, you full?"

She shrugged. "They'll go straight to my hips."

"You don't *have* hips."

"Well I still don't want any."

"Are you sure?" Mink said. "I mean, it's up to you, but that bullshit shouldn't be on your radar."

"I'm sure," Meli said, shoving her hands between her knees.

I'd seen them, heard them, hated them during hours of group therapy in my outpatient program—the girls who cared about nothing except how small they could get.

"Delicious!" I said and bit into a second macaroon.

Meli watched me with a new coldness.

We monitored the street from the porch, me with my cigarette, Mink with her tea. The smell of green came like water from the trees. Mink hummed to herself, staring off.

"You really think it was someone else?" I said.

"Of course it was. Cam hasn't been around in years."

"His parents might still live here," I reminded her.

Mink sighed and rubbed her foot. "Okay, so he comes for a three-day visit, then leaves. I wouldn't worry about it."

That was Mink's way, not to worry about it. She was so good at looking right in front of her, never to the side, certainly never behind. Maybe it helped to have a kid, another body to shelter, clean, and feed. Maybe the daily effort of keeping your kid alive and all right helped you not feel guilty for anything you'd done before.

Meli banged open the screen door and announced: "A girl got saved by lions. This girl in Ethiopia—*listen*, Mom—she was kidnapped and then but lions came and guarded—you're not listening."

"Now I am. Where did you hear this…?"

"TV. The girl was kidnapped to get married even though she was only twelve. Some evil men kept her for a week in the Ethiopian countryside and were hitting her and the way she cried sounded like a baby lion cub, so lions found her, and they scared away the men, and they stood in a circle around the girl for a long time until the police came. Isn't that so *good*, Mom?"

Mink agreed that it was.

"I *love* lions. They are incredibly smart. Do you love them, Quinn?"

"Well, sure," I said.

"In America," she added, "it would be done by wolves, since no lions are on this continent."

"What about bears?" said Mink.

"Maybe, but definitely wolves. The pack would encircle me until you got there. And one little wolf would be away from the pack being lonely until I talked to it and then it would go back to the circle and be okay."

She had come out of Mink's body. This person with her own curiosity—she had pushed blood-wet into the oxygen, made of pipes and wires, hinges and holes.

EDINBURGH LANE WAS a prewar house that didn't have air-conditioning.

"I'm all sweaty," I said. "I can't get comfortable."

"Once you're asleep, you won't notice," Fod said.

I wore just underwear. My sister and I got to be on the sunporch, where it was more outside, because our room upstairs was hottest. Our brother could hear us down there, through the floor. Not separate words but the voices, fighting. Crickets were scrizzing so loud it got in the way. Then she laughed, and I laughed. But after a while the fight voices started again.

Was she still mad when she went to sleep? No—she had been laughing. We were so sweaty we had to laugh. She was happy there was no school the next day. She fell asleep smiling. No, that's not true. I called her whiny little bitch and she turned away, shoulder in the air, on the squeaky sleeper-couch mattress. Stop pinching me I want to sleep. But she turned back again, before sleep. And did she smile? Yes she smiled. We were laughing. There was no school the next day.

In the morning, Riley craned on his toes to see inside the batter bowl. "What kind what kind—"

"Settle down," Mert said, "they're raisin."

Raisin was so boring.

"Go wake the big ones," she told Riley, "it's almost nine."

"They're being lazy," Riley said, hoping Mert would add something critical about us but she said nothing, went on stirring, reached to adjust the blue flame. Riley sniffed at the butter about to melt: angels' blood.

"Go on," our mother said.

We were still lazing. Two sheeted lumps on the porch bed. Riley yelled a magic yell that sometimes worked with my sister because she sometimes knew things before Riley said them. I didn't. It was because, she said, I had a dwarfed attention span. She was writing a story called "The Girl Too Poor to Pay Attention"; she had shown the first page to us. The girl was beautiful yet crippled from a Ferris wheel accident, which meant she couldn't work and had no money to pay the weekly attention.

"Guys," Riley said, "it's pancakes." He hit my legs, and I grunted; he leaned onto her legs to poke the feet. They didn't move. He poked again. Couldn't tell if she was faking; her face was hidden by the sheet.

"Tickle," I advised.

"Okay I'll be lieutenant." The lieutenant was responsible for holding down the victim while the captain tickled.

"Okay *go!*"

Riley pulled the sheet off our sister and it was all red, red, red, everywhere, like a smashed sun.

So will you switch places now? Okay, but only this one time.

"Did you wake them?" said our mother.

"No."

"No?"

"She won't get up," said Riley.

"Which one?"

"She has her period."

Mert swung around from the stove, her mitted hand on the skillet.

"And it's all over everything."

Mert set the skillet down. "What are you talking about?" She jumped forward and was gone. Riley picked up the red mitt from the linoleum. He would be helpful by putting it back on the counter, safely far from the flame.

Our mother came in saying, "*I'll* get her up, if you two can't . . . "

Then she yelled.

Then she fell.

"Mert," Riley said, "wake up." He pulled at her shoulders. When she saw Riley's hovering face, she started to yell again. Riley decided we must leave the porch at once to save Mert's eyeballs from the sight of her red daughter. "Let's," he said.

I was pressed to the fly-stuck screen, my white stomach with its furry black line heaving, underwear bunched at the tops of my thighs.

Riley said, "Let's."

I wanted to move. Nobody did. The air was going black and sweet—blacker and sweeter the longer we stood there—as the raisin pancakes burned away in the kitchen. It seemed impossible that a thing that had started *before* our mother knew her daughter was dead could still be happening *after*. The pancakes went on. They blackened blacker. I saw Riley's face twitch at the stink.

I RANG MY brother's bell, thinking to take him out to dinner, or at least to eat with him a dinner whose check we would split. I found him at tea with the limey. They were working with actual teacups. There was even a plate of what appeared to be scones; I picked one up.

"Help yourself," remarked Pine.

Riley, I noticed, had done something new to his mane. A product had been used: pomade? brilliantine? The straight fawn hairs, which normally fell in a hush, were clumpy and darker—almost bonafide spruce.

"Pine baked those," he said of the lemony charm in my mouth.

"You're a good cook," I said, knuckling crumbs off my lip.

Riley asked her, "Have you had a chance to talk to the intern yet? I forget his name."

"Blaze," Pine supplied.

"Is he, like, smart at all?"

"Don't know," said Pine, "but I *do* know that he suffers from halitosis."

"Do you, um, think he's attractive?"

Pine shrugged, reaching for the teapot. "If you like the dumb good health of a wheat thresher."

My brother looked so relieved I was embarrassed. I hoped Pine was flattered. Riley was kind of a plonker, but he was *true*. You got what you saw. Pine herself was off enough that perhaps it would be a heavenly match. She looked Riley's age, even though she talked like an elderly. I pictured her hometown as a hutted hamlet in stony green countryside, sheep agraze on every hill; her parents kept a shop; her childhood had been unspectacularly lonely.

Would our sister have smelled it on Riley, this oil of terrified desire? She had been able to smell in a classroom on test day the dread seeping off the students who hadn't studied. I had walked unprepared into my honors English final and quietly sniffed my armpit, but the sweat was gray-pink, as usual.

I went to pee, and when I returned, Riley was regaling Pine with the story of the ides of February. "The festival started," he said, "with the sacrifice of two male goats and a dog. Then two young priests were anointed upon the altar with the sacrificial blood, and the red knife was wiped with milk-soaked wool. Afterward was a feast, during which the Luperci priests (that means 'brothers of the wolf') cut thongs (which were called *februa*) from the carcasses of the sacrificed animals and, draped in goatskins, ran around the old city wielding the thongs. Girls and young women lined up to be lashed. Lashing was supposed to prevent sterility, ensure fertility, and ease childbirth pain."

"Sounds flipping terrible," Pine said.

"But it's *cool*, kind of…?"

She shrugged—"I am a sheltered village child"—and stood up, put a hand on my brother's shoulder. "Thank you for the tea. See you in the bunker tomorrow. Maybe the Afghan for lunch?"

While Riley saw her to the door, I finished the scone he must have been too nervous to eat. He got busy with the dishes. I was impressed all over again, from the back, by his hair. Dishes racked, he wiped down the table, cabineted the Lapsang souchong box, and lathered his pale hands with cucumber soap from a push-down dispenser.

"Want to grab some dinner?" I said.

He dried his hands on a towel embroidered with avocadoes. "We just ate."

"Yeah, but scones don't count."

"I'm not hungry."

"Okay, cool." But I didn't want to go. "Then I'll see you—soon?"

"Soon," he agreed, walking me to the door.

On my flat bed, I lay in nobody's arms. If an arm had been here, where would it have gone? Under my neck, like this; around my waist, like that. Up from the fog shot a high-school phrase: *Should we be quieter?*—Cam nodding at the ceiling, where my parents were. No, it's fine, they can't hear us. His self-consciousness had disappointed me. Such a tepid, piffling worry. *But what if we—But what if you—*Then I'll get it sucked out, I said. (Relief face.) Or I'll have it, and we'll buy an aerodynamic stroller. (Alarm face.) Don't joke about that! He had feared the most obvious threats. The only not-predictable thing was his clean skin. Not a single drop of ornament. It had made him stand out in a land of painted people.

My hands moved south, skimming acorn nipples, dough stomach. Back up to the padded shoulders, which used to feel knobbly. Down again to the thighs: one of these was nearly two of its former self. I'd had legs the width of icicles; my belly had sloped inward and could hold a boy's head; my hips had been holes for berries of bone.

"**BUT IT'S JUST** her period," Riley said. "Don't worry."

"No no no," said our mother.

"It's just she bleeds every month."

"Shut up," said Mert. "Shut up."

"But—"

"Shut *up*!"

Riley put a fist to his mouth.

Mert said, high-voiced, "It's not her period."

"She isn't dead!" shrieked Riley.

"Shut up," she said.

"She just forgot to wear a pad."

"Goddammit, Riley!"

"No, but she's—"

"Make him shut up," Mert wailed.

"Come here, Coyote," I said and crushed his face to my chest. "Be quiet, okay?"

"But she's *not*," said Riley into the bang of my heart. "I need to go check if she's still having her period."

I put my palm on his head. "No, stay here." His hair felt hot, like at the beach.

Mert dialed, then stared at the receiver. "You," she sputtered.

I took the phone. At my father's friendly "Yello?" I started to cry.

"Pettle? What's wrong?"

"Um, Fod?"

"What happened? Where's your mother?"

I pushed the receiver back at Mert, who told him to come home.

There was nothing to do. The police wouldn't let anyone on the sunporch. When Riley cuddled against me, his arm was so warm I wanted to shove it away; I was too sweaty myself to stand getting sweated on; but I was supposed to protect him. I couldn't protect, but I could let him press himself to me, soft in his T-shirt. Neither of us cried but Mert was crying and walking around and I prayed for Fod to hurry the fuck back from campus.

The worm nibbles the prisoner.

The worm carries my sister's eye in its mouth.

A piece of red was blackening on my elbow.

Fod got there after the ambulance, which was still parked out front since there was no hurry. A detective had come too, and other people—I didn't know what they did—who were looking around on the porch. Mert wouldn't let them interview us, so Riley and I were just sitting on the couch when Fod ran through the front door shouting "What? What is it?" He stood with his hands out in front of him. "Where's your mother?"

Riley said: "My sister died."

"Don't joke about that. Where's your mother?"

"No, she did."

I shoved my palms into my eyes.

Fod said, "What the hell is going on here?" and ran to the kitchen.

SAW THE GHOST *again. She was my sister's face, full of eyes. Not threat but not friend either. She was sizing up. Seeing what has become of me. And not snow, worse than snow, a kind of knifey rain. We could barely drive this morning. Stopped at gas station to fix wipers. Whose magnificent idea was it to book the Midwest in the middle of winter? said C and I whose idea (as he well knew) it was said Next time feel free to do all the booking yourself! and he wants me to tell him again why I got rid of Seven because if we had a manager we wouldn't be on this fucked route and I remind him for thousandth time that Seven was a thief and did he want a thief booking our shows? and C goes: If he sent us to Florida, then yes.*

IN A TRIBE, you knew your place. You knew you'd be taken care of, no matter what the weather. There was no lighting out for the territory, no lonely-hero journey into the abyss; the tribe enfolded you, smothering or comforting but always a net. In a tribe your worth was measured by connection—what you contributed to the whole—rather than by solitary achievement. You were judged *as part of.* No spotlights had trained white stares on me alone; their bodies had always been looked at, too. When we played in the mountains of the West, the air was so dry we dug fingernails into our nose walls to dislodge the solid cakes and blew red bits into napkins. The lack of oxygen made me sing better, because my voice didn't need to try so hard. I didn't drink my lemon that night, or the second night, or the third when we came down from the mountains onto a thousand-mile highway that rode through nothing. What mountains: Colorado? New Mexico? Some far place where folk called red and green salsa together Christmas and smiled at you for no reason. In the steep altitude my pens had burst, so I fingerprinted Cam's and Geck's faces and would have done Mink's too but she said, "Do you know how hard I work to keep toxins away from my skin?"

Like having a family better than the one you were born with. I had felt protected in their midst, not because any one of us was especially brave but because together, somehow—if we were together—we would always be okay. Calamity or curse might befall us, but no one would be lost.

Tribeless, I prepared my face for the day, and my mood happened to be good. In the toothpaste-crusted mirror my eyes looked less baggy than usual; the hike to the subway felt just one minute long; the toast in my hand was delicious. Hot blue wind, clean sky, everything beleafed a silver-green—not a bad morning to be ankling the earth. On the train I stared at the kids with white veins dangling from their ears, sending brain juice to jacket pockets. Cups tucked into the pockets—slender, flat cups—collected the juice, saved it for later. A bonny boy noticed me (repeated head adjustments across the plastic aisle) and I was proud of myself for not being too pitifully glad about it.

It would be a good day—it *would*.

Up the bleached concrete trail from the subway station, up the little slope. I'd buy Ajax lunch and tell him to pack it in early, go fetch his monsters from day care.

"How many cocoa patties will you desire today?" I yelled back to the office.

"No, man, I'm…"

"What's that?"

"I said no thanks."

"But, my treat!"

Ajax emerged, staring at his hand. "Got something to discuss."

The sign on the door hadn't been turned to OPEN, though it was quarter past. He leaned his elbows on the counter and opened his palm: the wooden ear-arrow, dark with blood. I looked up at his torn lobe. A second before he said the words, I heard them, so that the sentence felt like echo: "We have to close the store."

"Oh, crap—" I reached for my pack.

"I'm gonna file for Chapter 7. Man, I'm sorry, I waited long as possible to tell you, thought it might not happen, some kind of miracle would—"

"Maybe my parents can loan us some," I said.

"Yeah, they really have that kind of cash. Mine don't either."

Scraping the match, I noticed, as if from a great distance, that my thumb was shaking. "How long more will we—"

"Not long."

"I'm sorry," I said.

"Nobody's fault," Ajax said.

SHE HAD BLED all over herself. Blood fell out in the night. Dumb sister you didn't bandage it up. It goes between your legs and the sheet is red forever and you could've gotten blood on me and you *did*—a little patch.

Our mother said, "Oh Christ" and I looked where she was looking, at my elbow, and licked my thumb but Mert shouted, "Leave it!"

I had my sister on me.

She had her period all over herself, and had gotten some on my elbow.

"It's from between her legs," Riley said, and our father took his cheeks in his fingers, hard.

"Don't Fod I'm sorry," he whispered.

Mert said, "Not from *there*, baby—from her head."

My sister could smell in a girl's mouth if she was bleeding.

The police took the sheets and the pillow. T-shirt and underwear would be cut from her body later. They strung yellow tape around the porch and said to keep away.

"But we have to clean that floor," Mert said.

"No, ma'am, please don't clean anything."

"But the floor," she said.

The detective nodded. "I know, ma'am. There'll be plenty of time to clean it, but please, not yet. Forensics team still needs to get in there." Puffs of skin were darkening under his eyes. He would be back, he told my parents. "Please try to get some rest."

"Thank you," Fod said roughly, and shook his hand.

THE BABY TENTACLE was swollen today, red at the rim of the nail. The clerk's mood seemed no worse; he rang up my aspirin with his usual tranquil efficiency; but if the tentacle was infected he must have been in some pain.

"How's it going?"

"Fine," squeaked Two Thumbs, "you?"

"Sick of this rain."

"Right?" he said but was, as usual, in no mood for small talk, and looked past me to the next customer. I muttered thanks and swung out with my purchases. The old white lady with her red-painted wrinkles nodded as we passed. In all the years I had lived on this street we'd never spoken, but she usually offered an unsteady smile. She had a plastic hood over her hair, face open to the downpour. Why wasn't the blush running down her cheeks? Red stain on elbow. I had licked my finger and gone to wipe it, but Mert shouted No. I'd had my sister on me—a little patch of her.

Before long I was walking into the old neighborhood, where you couldn't spit without hitting a spark or two. I blinked at the neon sign of a new computer café where the radio station had once stood. Nobody could see me. They all passed without seeing. Umbrellas, running faces. The tether strained, frayed, unraveled; and when I went fully deaf, it would snap. That hitchhiker in Portland had been deaf, but hadn't seemed too sad about it. Had been, in fact, a rather cheerful guy. How the dickens could he have felt cheerful when he went around in a box of silence? But he had laughed freely, offered us pieces of a spicy chocolate bar, and winked at Mink when her shirt caught on the van door *by accident of course* and opened before his very eyes.

My feet kept moving. I was swerving onto Belfry Street. Under the trees the water, gushing off leaves, hit me harder. There were no cactus pots on the porch; the widow's walk railing was bare. Our flag had flown the whole time we lived on Belfry Street, years of comings and goings—only Cam and I had remained constant inhabitants—different bodies in the bedrooms, different snack preferences and television habits and degrees of substance abuse.

I lit one from the new pack. Wet asphalt hissed under tires. The churches waited heavily in their places. I was tired of walking around, but the bar didn't open for another three hours. So I circled back toward the trees. Down in the park, branches guarded against sky. Pine brooms on the gravel path, a piece of string, flares of old weed, a puddle grown over with prismy oil. I sat for a while on a dead tree, its stump sliced to expose a moss-rimmed butthole.

THE SUMMER WENT on, even though her body had stopped. The leftover children were amazed to watch the air get wetter and the trees greener; to hear cheers from playing fields; and to see the yellow moon.

Three weeks after the middle's funeral, they drove downtown for fireworks. The oldest had her period. She thought about how this very same gloppy red mucous had been inside her when her sister was alive, growing dark on the walls of the bag only inches away from her sister's gang of eggs when they lay together on the porch. In those eggs had been the nieces and nephews the oldest would have taught to play guitar.

She hoped a misaimed rocket would explode into the statue of the famous explorer, killing at least a few of the crowd.

The mother handed her a plastic pouch of juice with its own puncturing straw. Fifteen is too old for juice, thought the oldest, sucking, shame a gray sleeve on her lung. Red broke in the black air. The youngest asked,

"Can the fireworks fall on us?"
     The family was four.

"**QUINN, I KNOW** you don't love to talk about this, but I've noticed, we've both noticed, that you've dropped a little bit of weight recently. I'm only bringing it up because I want to—to—to check in with you. Is everything all right?"

Mert had learned *check in* from the good doctor during the bad times.

"Yeah fine," I said.

"Really," I said.

"I've been walking more," I said, "now that the weather's nicer, maybe that's—"

"Well, you want to keep an eye on it, right?"

"An eye is being kept."

My parents smiled and sipped their waters, but in the bad times, they had screamed: *You will.* I won't. You will. I won't. Yes, Quinn, you will. No I fucking *won't*. What did you say to me? Nothing, Fod, I'm sorry. You're going to eat what is on that plate. No. Goddammit, Quinn, put it in your mouth and chew. No. Why are you doing this to yourself? Answer me! *No.* Yes. No. You—will—put—this—in—your—mouth—*Leave* it, Will! from where she'd stood at the stove; Mert hadn't even wanted to be in the same room. Just leave her alone. But later, in the night kitchen, she had said, Darling girl, what goes on inside your head? in such a wrecked voice my eyes ached. I'd said, My thoughts, I guess. If you don't eat, you are going to die. I eat, I shrugged, which launched a fresh surge of scream: *When?* When do you eat? At school? On the bus? I certainly never see you do it! Your father never sees you do it! When could you possibly be eating if you look like—Mert stood back, bumping hard into the stove—*that!*

At first the good doctor, who I went to after those failed sessions with the dink, had been barking up the wrong tree. "Does being thin make you feel powerful? When your mother tries to make you eat, and you refuse, how do you feel?" I answered every question truthfully, and the good doctor seemed confused. When the first visit ended she told me she was most intrigued, and at the next appointment, instead of hammering away in the same old direction as the dink had, she switched tacks.

"And who is the bloodworm?"

"Worm who eats blood and is made of blood."

"Where does the worm come from?"

"Underneath," I said.

"Underneath what?"

"Just underneath."

"Why are you afraid of the bloodworm?"

"It ate my sister."

She could smell in a forest if a wolfberry grew.

"How do you know?"

"I see it."

"You mean you saw it?"

"No, *see.*"

The good doctor paused, then said, "You have recurring mental images of this worm consuming your sister's flesh?"

I nodded.

"And where else does the bloodworm live?"

I shook my head.

The good doctor asked again.

"Down there," I said. "It eats the blood."

"Down where, Quinn?"

"When your period comes," I hissed.

"Does the worm live in your vagina?"

"*No!*" I was furious but couldn't explain. In and out of my sister's holes. Eyes, mouth, ears, downstairs. A snail shell isn't big enough for your whole ear—you can't get the ocean. Try with two. *I still can't.*

"Please don't worry," I told my mother now. "I'm eating enough. I seriously am."

Mert smiled faintly. "Okay."

"*Promise* you won't worry?"

"Promise," she said.

"Death tolls went up again this month," Fod said.

"November can't come soon enough. Get that lunatic out of the White House…"

"He might win again," I said.

"There is no way that imbecile—that *ambulatory lobotomy* could win again."

"But he might."

"I assure you, kid, he won't."

I said, "You know who would've loved that term, ambulatory lobotomy? *She* would have."

Mert said, "I think that's enough, Quinn, don't you?"

"I've only had two glasses!"

"Three, in fact," she said.

"Wine is good for you," I pointed out, continuing to pour. "There was this study that said it prevents heart disease."

"I just think"—Mert's voice was at its carefulest—"that you're going through a challenging time, with the job loss, and it might be a good idea not to drink so much."

I laughed. "I *don't* drink that much. You should see some of my associates! Like remember Jonathan Geck? By the way, thanks for dinner, it was really good…" I itched to be gone, but there was still the after-meal tea.

"Earl Grey or English Afternoon?"

"Shock me," I said.

The lagging hours of *being together*. God bless them, they tried, but the trying felt sad. Why?—because I was supposed to have a family of my own by now, or starting one? Because I came by myself across town for these

dinners, a stunted oldening girl who still wished the television were on as a buffer? I had broken my rubber-band
bracelet on the bus and was reluctant to hunt for another in the kitchen with Mert around. She might have
offered some comment on my life, how it was not much
of one. Instead I latched myself into the hall bathroom
and held my wrists under the cold until they were gone.
Only boring people get bored, Mert used to say when we
complained how long Saturday was without TV. My sister said, But that's an *ipse dixit*! Dogmatic and unproven
statement, she added to me, and I yelled, You mean they
made up a whole term specially for Mert? and Mert
sneered: Do you even know what dogmatic means? Yeah,
I said, it means the way you talk.

"Squidling?" she called. "Milk or lemon?"

"Lemon," I shouted, wiping numb fingers on the
reindeer towel. How could they still have this ancient
rag? Riley had worn it as a cape when our sister made
him be demented elf.

Mert watched me slurp at the kitchen table, her own
teacup untouched. I wondered where my brother was—
must've had better things on tap tonight, though what
that little monk could possibly have had on tap was a
mystery. Fod? Out plucking a few more hairs from his
garden. And where was *she*? Like smoke around us, sighing at the crinkled shells of our ears.

"Please let your father drive you back," Mert said and
I nodded, even though it meant twenty more minutes of
eyes. If Riley had been here we would have dropped him

off first (the paranoia law didn't count for short trips inside the city) then continued on to my neighborhood where my father always locked the car doors. After our sister died, no more than two of us—one parent, one kid—could take a car journey or fly in a plane together. It had made vacations complicated. We'd bought a second car, a used hatchback whose seats had smelled like guinea pig. I'd hated the law, but Riley had agreed it was a good idea to make sure some people were left over.

Tonight the streets were quiet, traffic lights changing without any cars. I turned on the radio hoping to find noise that did not demand attention—a newscast, for instance, in a foreign language. I stopped on an army recruitment commercial.

"Why didn't Ri come tonight?"

"He already had plans with someone," Fod said. "A classical music concert, I think."

"A *date*?"

"Is that so outrageous?"

"Well."

Be! All that you can—!

"Your mother mentioned a girl who…"

"What's that?"

"A girl who works at the archives."

We were nearing the intersection where Fod would press the automatic lock. The radio said "And now a blast from the past!" and out jumped the opening bars of "Dear Done For," clackety drums, ping ping ping of guitar, slim thump of bass. *Fod, this is us!* I wanted to reach for the dial but my arm wouldn't. My father didn't recognize the song. The music coiled into a long, narrow tube. My vision was zooming. If your head lost enough blood, you passed out. The lack of oxygen turned off the brain, and a fight-or-flight response kicked in: all blood rushed to the torso to protect your heart, so you had no blood in your legs either, making a collapse even more likely. The remedy the good doctor had taught me was to stick my head between my knees, as if bracing for a plane crash. But I couldn't do this in front of Fod. I couldn't see except straight in front. My blood was marching for my heart, leaving the brain dry and alone. My sister had lost all her blood too. Her skull had been drained of gore, membrane shriveled, salt gone.

On his date my brother would have worn dark stiff denim, hoping Pine couldn't tell the britches were new. In the night air, colder than he'd planned for, his windbreaker would have been like paper.

Maybe once, with her. Just once. After once, it would have been over, not regretted but never spoken of again. In the Caribbean there grows a kind of cactus whose flowers bloom only one night a year, carry out their sex lives, and are dead by morning.

"My favorite was the flute," he told Pine.

"Mine was the oboe," she said, "although I wouldn't want to meet an oboe player in a dark alley." Pine did the trick of making her eyes go in different directions.

"Stop that with your eyes!"

She shut them obediently and Riley thought, Now would be a good time. When she's not looking. But they opened again. Maybe when they were back in their neighborhood, at the intersection where she went left and he went right?—maybe then he would do it. He was the boy, after all.

"Thank you for the concert," she said as they got off the bus. "It was brilliant."

"I'm glad you liked it," said Riley.

"Thank you," she repeated at the corner where he went right and she went left.

"You're welcome."

They stood apart, arms hanging.

"Well," she said, "I shall see you Monday."

He waved and smiled, the virgin youngest.

A BULLET IS a mouthful of pennies. A bullet tears metal and meat. A bullet shot on the night of June 2, 1984, went through my sister's head and they found it later on the floor. It carried, the forensic tests would show, tiny pieces of her hair, skin, and brain. We had been sleeping with our heads to the window. The glass was up. The bullet made a hole in the screen. They threw away the screen. They patched the skull for burial so the brains couldn't climb. Fod wanted her cremated but Mert said they weren't burning her girl.

"We have to clean the floor. The floor has got to be cleaned. We need soap and a bucket."

We watched our mother move in little swipes around the kitchen, looking for things in the air, muttering, "That floor in there. It really can't stay like that. We have to fix it."

"Coo," I said.

"Coo," finished Riley.

"Why are you two just *standing* there," Mert mumbled,

opening a cabinet. She stood for a long time looking at
the shelves.

"Are you going to start cooking again?" I asked.

"What?"

"*Cooking*, Mert, like when you take food and make
it hot?"

> Lacustrina dreamt of sharks, who needed
> salty sea—her lake had water fresh as rain
> where no small sharks could be. She dreamt
> she met an octy in the driftings of a wreck;
> he wrapped his sucking tentacle around her
> tender neck. Awake she gathered twirlshell
> snails and put them in her basket. When she
> had a question, she wasn't scared to ask it.

Why did Mr. Walker keep a pistol? Why did stupid goddamn Mr. Walker keep a pistol in his stupid goddamn
house? Why did Mr. Walker have to get it, and cock it,
and fire it six times at the goddamn kid? The burglar
was not even voting age. Fod did not blame the burglar,
who'd had no weapon. He blamed Bill fucking Walker
that gun-loving Republican who had seen fit like the
fuckface he was to keep a pistol in his kitchen drawer.

Don't say fuckface, don't say fuckface, said the back
of my mouth, but he kept saying it and from the bathroom Mert screamed, "If I hear that word one more
time I'm going to kill myself!"

I explained to Riley what a figure of speech was.

I was peeling my fingers, seeing how long the strips of skin could go. I had three peels laid out already on the coffee table. Fod saw. "Disgusting," he shouted. "You're fifteen years old, stop acting like a baby."

If Walker showed up to the funeral, I planned to slice his throat. I sharpened my army knife the night before. Riley, watching me scrape its blade on a stone from the yard, said: "But then you have to go to jail."

I said I didn't care and besides I was a minor so the sentence would be short.

"Why isn't Mr. Walker in jail?" asked Riley.

I shrugged. I'd duct-taped a cotton sheath to the inside of my dress so I could bring the knife out quickly, before Walker knew what was happening. In the throat I would cut him. The funeral home would have to get a new carpet.

"ENCORE," I SAID from the end of the bar. Mink poured me a fifth, a sixth. "My tab," I nodded, though there had never been a tab. I scratched the sleeve of red and black, a dragon and a sailor's ghost and a doll with crimson eyes. Nearby hovered venereal Lad. He was playing later, down the street, in the terrible band helmed by Geck. Who still had his hopes. It was impressive, really. After all these hundreds of years, he was still making a go.

"You nervous?" I bellowed at Lad.

"I don't get nervous," he said.

The junior bartender said, "Oh listen to you." She was at the taps with her shoulders wrenched back, thrusting every inch of mammary gland into the sky.

He grinned her way. Lad liked to sleep with barely legals and to exaggerate for them the length of a brief prison term he had served back when they were still trading puffy stickers. This salty rooster had bedded half the young ladies in town—including, in the old days, if we are being entirely honest, myself.

When I pushed my empty glass at her, Mink elbowed it aside and leaned forward. She said, "I need to show you something."

"Can you show me *after* you get me another drink?"

"No."

Other than Lad, now having a giggle attack with the junior bartender, there were no other customers.

"Well, what?"

From her back pocket she pulled a crumple of newspaper and flattened it on the silver bar. It was a tiny article, one cramped paragraph, and my eyes were blurring; I had to squint. I saw the name of the university where my parents taught, and the word *appoints*, and Cam's name.

"He was appointed…?" I groped.

"A visiting professor," Mink explained, "at the law school. For one semester."

"Why would he teach at a law school?"

"Because he's a *lawyer*."

"Cam would never be a lawyer," I declared.

"Read it yourself," she said. "He's a tax attorney in Seattle."

FOR HIS FIRST-EVER photo project, my brother had stolen pictures from Mert's closet box and photocopied them. He cut three different versions of our sister (laughing on the sunporch, frowning in the tree house, eating a slice of sugar cake) and glued them on a page. Photocopied again. Again cut them, this time chopping the sisters into halves and arranging them on a new page. Again copied.

The result was, to him, mesmerizing.

He bought a frame at the drugstore. He went to Belfry Street and showed it to Cam, who said too quickly: "That's really good." Riley's snake photograph was already on a nail in the red hall; he hoped we might want to hang this up, too. When I came home, he waited for me to notice what was leaning on the mantel of the not-working fireplace. I brushed the rabbit off the couch so I could lie down. Finally Riley pointed and said, "Do you like it?" and I looked.

"No," I said.

"Oh," he said.

"Sorry," I said, "but it's kind of—obvious? Death, fragmentation, distortion, blah blah blew. I get it, but I don't *want* to get it so easily, you know?"

Cam was nicer. He paid attention. On Sundays at the diner he would instruct the waitress: "This one will have the *rye* toast, please!" and Riley loved the pun. On the bed Cam asked, "Do you have a crush on anyone?" and Riley, facedown on black sateen, mumbled no.

"Oh, come on, there must be somebody. In your grade? Any cute girls?"

Riley rolled over onto his back. "No, not really."

"Aha!" Cam lit a cigarette, shook the match. "Not really means yes."

"Oh, no, I meant not really as in there aren't really any cute girls at…"

"Get your hand off your mouth!" He pulled Riley's fingers away. "Now *what'd* you say?"

"I don't like anyone," my brother said.

BEFORE DIALING HIS number I imagined Geck, golden mane and dents in his cheeks, belly astrain against polyester loungewear. He'd probably left his meeting early tonight. His mother went to the bother of cooking supper, the least he could do was not make them wait to eat it! When he limped in, she would ask her usual How was it, sweetie? and he would answer his usual Same. Worse, he might add, enraged by how relieved she looked.

He would reach the spaghetti bowl down from its shelf, lay out three tomato place mats, a good son.

The bowl he had left for her several months ago had not been a good-son bowl. The guest bathroom packed to its porcelain gills, brimming with at least four sits' worth of runny dump he'd been too dodge-sick to bother to flush—imagine her delight. It was possible she had not discovered the diarrhea until days after they'd driven him to Canterbury, by which time the stink— well, yeah. She'd never said one word. She would visit him on Sundays with foil-covered puddings and crisps.

These he had chosen not to share with the other patients.

"Supper in five minutes!" his mother said, and he sat up with effort, punching off the blanket. His leg was killing. Where was the penis cane? He'd need it soon. He was forty on a flowered couch.

They had just hit the table, napkins lapped, spoon driven into the pile of red-sauced spaghetti, when the phone rang.

"Telemarketers," his mother said dejectedly.

"Leave it go," his father said. "Those criminals need to learn you don't interrupt people while they're eating."

Geck rose, shaking out his stiff knee. "Someone could've died," he pointed out.

"Oh, Jonathan…"

"Hospitals notify day and night. Speak!" he crooned into the receiver.

"Hello."

"Quinn?"

"Am I interrupting anything?"

"Shit no," he said. "What's up?"

"I wanted to tell you something," I said.

"What, that you can't curtail your sexual daydreams of me?"

"Shut up. It's Cam. He's back."

"**IF THE PRESIDENT** had died from the bullet, would you have cried?"

"*Cheered.*"

"I wouldn't cry either," said the youngest, "but I don't think he should be dead, maybe."

"Quinn's just saying that," said the middle, "because Mert and Fod hate the president—she doesn't know crap about him."

"Are you kidding me," said the oldest, "I read the newspaper!"

"CRAZY-TOWN," GECK AGREED. "Are you going to call him?"

"What? No."

"We could organize a reunion."

"Are you serious?"

"Wull, I mean, why not? Have a few cold ones; reminisce."

"The terms on which we parted," I reminded him, "were not happy terms."

"He might've forgotten by now."

"Geck, he lost every single finger on his left hand."

"So? He's had time to get used to it. Maybe his nickname is Fisty."

Why had I gone looking for water in the driest of wells?

"THE IRONY OF it," our father said. "The fucking irony." We watched the moving men tie blankets around the dining-room table. The August sky was hard white. I kept my hands in my pockets. "Moving *into* the city to get—" But Fod didn't say *safer* because that wasn't really the right word. We were moving to get away from the house, from the neighborhood. My parents had chosen Edinburgh Lane in the first place because the public schools were better out there; now nobody gave a crap about schools. When Riley asked, "Where am I going to go?" Mert whispered, "That's not important right now!"

But it was to Riley. And to me, though I didn't say, because it was embarrassing to worry about a new school when you were as old as tenth grade. Coyote could worry, because he was only starting sixth. He insisted: "What school will I go to?"

"I have no idea," Mert said.

"When will you have an idea?"

"Goddammit," she said, "I don't know."

"But next month is September."

"Riley, this isn't the time, it really isn't—"

"When *will* be the time, Mert?"

I admired him.

On our second morning at Observatory Place, Riley licked me awake. "Come down," he whispered, tugging my wet ear. In the front room was a television more massive than any of my friends had. We stood shocked. The house law had always been none whatsoever. Rots the gray matter, Fod said, and Mert said, You have better things to do with your lives.

"Now if a plane falls into the river we won't have to go next door," Riley pointed out.

I was thinking only of the music channel—videos after parents asleep—

"Squidlings, this is not going to be a free-for-all," Mert announced at breakfast in her most clenched voice. "There will be limits, but…" She looked at Fod.

"We thought it might help everyone relax," he explained.

It was a bigger basement than Edinburgh Lane's, though the house itself was smaller because now we were four. I took the longest knife from the wood block and went down to slice the top box. I wanted my sister's notebooks, but this one had little shirts and jellies and ankle-zip britches. *Where you are going, clothes won't help.* They smelled like nothing, least of all trees. She'd had the better nose and I the better ears (or the worse, because in their acuteness they bothered me more). When she whispered *That man smells bad* she did not mean his odor, but that he did evils. She could smell in a yard if a cat's bones were buried there. She could smell at a bedroom door if the person who slept within had good dreams or sad. From the library she checked out a history of scent. *It was once believed, she copied into her notebook, illness could be detected from how a person smelled—that diabetes smelled of sugar; measles of freshly plucked feathers; the plague of mellow apples; inflamed kidneys of ammonia.* Yellow fever smells of the butcher shop! she sang in the kitchen, watching Mert pare white rinds off pink meat.

"WILL MY BREASTS be bigger than yours?"

"Pardon me?"

"When I'm a teen," Mink's daughter explained.

"Only time will tell," I said.

"Yours are really small."

I'd liked her better before she learned to speak.

"Small but fierce!" I said.

Meli squinted. "How can a breast be fierce? I think mine will be big since my mom's are. Do you think I should get a bra?"

"You're eight."

"A girl in my class has a training."

I laughed. "What would it be holding up on you?"

"*You* wear one," she said.

"I need to go ask your mother something."

I was sitting on the toilet when Mink wrenched the bath taps, groped for a towel.

"What the eff," she said. "Why are you in here?"

"She was insulting me."

Mink hollered toward the door: "We need to leave in five minutes, okay?"

A faint yell of assent.

She patted the towel up between her thighs. The summer I caught the glingles from Lad, Mink had been ready with instructions. It wasn't a big deal, she had explained, if you cleaned downstairs with a medicated soap.

"Insulting you?"

"No, nothing. I just came in to say hello."

She stared into the cloudy mirror, fingering her forehead. "I have new wrinkles."

"Don't be a cliché," I said.

"That line was *not there* before."

"Don't be a wife-magazine article."

"Oh, like you never worry about it? I read about this eye cream," she went on, "that naturally unclenches the skin so that it lets go of each wrinkle—but it's sixty-five dollars a jar. I have to buy her summer clothes soon, she's growing out of everything. She wants to go to sleepaway camp because her two best friends are. *That's* not going to happen, let me assure you. Two minutes!" she shouted.

No response.

"Did you hear me, Meli?"

No response.

Mink slapped on lotion. "Of *course* you worry about it."

"I don't know where my fisher boots are," the girl complained through the door.

"Then wear your sneakers."

"I need my fisher boots."

"You don't need them, you *want* them. Different."

"Same!" she whined.

"The car is leaving," Mink said, "in one minute."

How was Mink going to be ready in one minute?

"Fine then I'm staying here."

"Put your fucking sneakers on!" yelled Mink.

In the truck, wipers churning, Meli between us blinked fast against her tears. Her lashes were tasselly. "Why's it raining again?"

"Because that's what it does," Mink said.

"But why?"

"Because the sky grasshoppers are taking their bath."

On the radio they were speculating about the Democrats' chances, the election mere months away, time at last to evict from the White House its death-happy emperor.

Meli reached for the dial.

"Wait," Mink said, "I want to hear this."

"But it's boring."

"It's *important*, because we have a bad situation on our hands."

"We do?"

"Remember we've talked about the war, and how so many people in the Middle East are dying—"

"Yeah I know but Mrs. Pargiter says we had to do it to topple the madman."

Mink's foot banged the brake.

"Why are we stopping?"

"She said the invasion of Iraq was *good*?"

"I don't know," Meli said carefully.

"Her teacher supports the war," Mink said to me. "That's fantastic."

Meli screeched, "Don't tell her I told you, she'll be mad at me, okay? *Okay*, Mom?"

"I won't, bee."

Mink's forehead-prodding vanity was understandable. Earned. In the day, she had been gorgeous in a way that made guys do extreme things. She'd once had a boyfriend who kept three of her pubic hairs in his pocket watch—a nod, only half jesting, to the medieval custom where a knight wore his lady's private locks into battle, a way to maintain the discretion required by courtly love—and Mink had liked that he did this, although when he first plucked and set aside the hairs she thought it was weird, didn't know him well enough yet to trust that he wasn't one of those guys who run used-panty mail-order businesses out of their basements. Sometimes, she told me later, they'd be sitting around with a bunch of people and he would take the watch from his pocket, rub it with his thumb, and smile at her.

I was not across-the-room beautiful. Never had I felt the way Mink had been able to feel on a regular basis: that your face and body forced eyes to go in a particular direction. A conjuring act, to have your shell be so arresting that all motion in other people was halted. I used to get furious—not at Mink, because it wasn't her fault, but at the fact that a girl's best weapon was her casing. Rare to run across one who played an instrument well enough to be noticed for the playing and not for how cute she looked while playing it. Voices, yes, could astonish—you'd find girl singers who used their vocal cords for paranormal purposes—but the cords were in their bodies; they were not foreign objects to be mastered. And for every hundred boys who played like crap, not masterly at all, there was a boy you could point to and say *He has powers,* whereas you could hardly ever point to a girl.

We licked soft-serve cones, supervising Meli's playground moves. "So he hasn't gotten in touch with you," I said.

"For the third time, no. And I doubt he will. It's already the middle of the semester." Mink yawned and tongued ice cream off her lower lip. She was able to switch her mind entirely to NOW. Give every inch of attention to her daughter's teacher, to a cone of ice cream, to refilling glasses of beer. For Mink, it seemed, there was no past. No guilt.

"And then in May or June he'll just, what, go back to Seattle? Just like that?"

"What else would he do?" she said.

DEAR CAM,

We wonder do you dye your hair because you look like you would naturally have lighter hair and you and Mink would make a great baby we think a Pure baby whereas the singer looks like a JEW. We know it is difficult to discuss these matters in the current climate of Pro-Semitism in this country but we feel you should know that you and Mink have our unwavering support and we hope that you will issue a child who can carry on the vital work of our Race. We are disappointed that you would play music with a JEW (or possibly two JEWS, we are not sure of the origins of the guitar player) so you would have our support in striking out on your own with Mink and forming a group which is more Pure. If you are interested in receiving additional information in addition to the literature we have enclosed, please contact us.

Yours in Struggle,

The Youth Corps of the
American Alliance for the
Preservation of Aryan Culture

YOU WERE A shipwrecked sailor. A plague had fallen upon your boat, and your sick mates, believing the sea was green fields, had been throwing themselves overboard. Water, water, everywhere. The delirious captain had just set the deck on fire and lain down screaming in the blaze. You, untouched by malady, floated alone on a life raft.

One by one the creatures arrived: a trio of dolphins, a baby octopus, a circling shark, a vulture dripping bits of illness from its beak. And one by one the hurdles: lightning, hailstorm, tidal wave. A computerized voice intoned: *Slimy things did crawl with legs upon the slimy sea. About, about, in reel and rout, the death-fires danced at night; the water, like a witch's oils, burnt green, and blue, and white.*

The joystick wasn't very good for swimming with, or ducking lightning, or plucking the pearl from its shell, which made it a maddening game—all this water and monster and weather and so little influence upon them. I was playing badly, drowned in the first round and eaten by a squid in the second.

COLD RAIN AND *we have no place as usual to be until tonight so we take our time finding break-fast wandering 5mph round cancergarden of a town nobody can agree on where. If I eat any more grease I will die of bad skin! is mantra of M who's got skin of Ukrainian supermodel and G keeps bitching he has no $ because we're not paying him enough and finally C who doesn't ever yell yells We never said we'd pay you so shut the fuck up!*

Finally we end up at some egg place econo enough for G and I wait for C to slide in beside me but he stands there until only seat left is way on other side of booth then digs in about sloppiness last night. We can't even order b/c he's droning on about this and that like, such as, M why do you keep going on the one in-stead of the two in Northern Direction? and

G stop growing your fucking hair, the solo in Floors is way too long! and nobody says anything because when he gets hatey there is no stopping him (so far, so usual) but then knives come for me: you sounded like you were choking last night, why aren't you drinking lemon, how can we even play if you sound like that? etc etc etc and M says I think you're being unfair which sends C on fresh roll—You always defend her why is that? Coalition of vaginas?—which pisses M off and she snipes at the waitress Where's our fucking ashtray? and I see clumps of fresh snot shot onto our breakfasts immediately before serving.

I'D SEEN A darkness on my underwear the night before, and hoped it was only from dinner. Asparagus made your pee smell so maybe it stained your underwear too. In the morning I couldn't pretend it was a vegetable's fault because the blood was so bright—a metal red on the sheet in the shape of a short, thick worm. Oh no oh no oh no. A burnt smell plugged my throat. Oh no. Her crusty eyes opened: *See?* and her voice said, The uterus is a pouch! and it said, A bullet is pennies in your mouth and a bullet tears flesh with the ease of a— I ripped the sheet from the bed, balled it, saw the worm had soaked through to the mattress pad so pried the pad off as well. The mattress showed a vague brownishness, hardly noticeable, but I flipped it over. Hid the sheet and mattress pad under the bed and tied a sweater around my waist. In the kitchen Mert asked what the trash bag was for and I said, A project. *See? See?* I kept the bag of stained cotton in my closet for three days until it was trash night, and waited until Fod had dragged the laden can to the curb before running out with my secret bag and stowing it at the very bottom, under the grinds and shells.

A bullet, depending on its angle of entry, can cleave the striations of a muscle in such a way as to trigger profuse hemorrhaging that is difficult, if not impossible, to stanch.

At the new school, my teachers were all fake-nice. They knew, of course. I felt eyes, eyes, eyes. I couldn't laugh or tell a joke because the eyes believed I was sad all the time. I wasn't, though—I was nothing. My skull made a room with nothing in it. My one worry was Riley, who was so shy. The middle school was three blocks away and I'd go over during lunch to see if I could see him. Be brave, Coyote, I would whisper at the windows.

Lunch was a relief because I could be alone, away from the eyes. I ate my sandwich outside and checked my teeth for lettuce in a parked car's mirror. There was one crew of boys I didn't hate. They were not like regular boys. They slouched darkly at the ends of halls, in tight britches and heavy boots, their hair pink or blue or black-black. The tall one was in English with me; his best friend, the hot one, wasn't in any of my classes. I stayed on the lookout but rarely saw the hot one. The only chance was at lunch, and the cafeteria had all those eyes.

I was The Girl Whose Sister Got Killed. They knew the story. They put me in honors English, where the teacher said: "Quinn is an interesting name."

I said not really, it was some dumb British relative's name.

"Are your parents British?" asked Mr. Nzambi.

I gouged at the desk with a pencil. Mr. Nzambi waited. When the silence got bad enough, a boy blurted: "Well everyone's parents are, *originally*," and Mr. Nzambi cleared his throat and a black kid said, "Except mine!" and another black kid said, "Yeah, or mine," and I felt bad for the boy, who sounded racist when he might not have been.

Mr. Nzambi moved on with attendance. When I looked up, the boy was watching me. I could not know—Cam told me only much later—that he pitied me because of my lame beige sweater.

WHEN I CALLED the law school, I disguised my voice. This was not, I knew, exactly necessary. In a choked rumble I said, "I'd like the mailing address of your visiting tax professor, Cameron—"

"Okay," the secretary said, and told me.

How could it be that easy?

Well, he wasn't a CIA agent.

"Thank you," I grunted, and noticed that my voice sounded like a cartoon dog's, and hung up the phone.

HE PASSED ME a scrap in Nzambi's class: *Want to go shopping after 8th?* It was better than going home. We took the bus downtown and went into a shop with glittering walls. A girl with shot-up hair stood at a mirror adjusting a white leather dress that did not even cover her whole butt, and I stared (until I remembered not to) at the scrumptious tuck where her netted thighs started.

Cam bent over the case of hair dyes, tapping his plastic rings on the glass. "Magenta or cobalt? What should I get?"

I said, "Isn't Pete's hair magenta?"

Cam frowned and ran over to a rack of fur.

I looked around cautiously, ashamed to be there in my regular shoes.

"Try these on," Cam said, returning with a pair of inky britches that were small enough for Riley.

"Won't fit."

"They're *stretch*," he explained.

I did not buy any garb that day; left the store with a small pin only; but I had memorized how the britches looked. How they made *me* look: hard and dark, as if I knew something.

For Christmas I asked for a record player and Fod said, But you listen to tapes. That's about to change, I said. Cam had a whole crate; some of them his cousin had put him onto, but many were his own finds—he spent hours after school and on Saturdays at the record store, laboring through the racks. He invited me one day to go and I agreed, hoping Pete would come too, but Cam showed up alone. The guy at the counter told me, With those eyes, you should be a tambourine player. I smiled but felt weird, and wondered why, an early blip of sensing that, as a girl, I was at an unnamed, unpointable-to disadvantage. Cam led me through the aisles. Have you heard I do you like I have you heard I shit they're amazing I have you heard I they're so overrated I *have you heard this shit?* and no, I hadn't heard much of any of it. But I planned to.

MY BROTHER HESITATED at the door, not a bar-goer. I pushed him through. I wanted to enjoy the evening, my treat to pay him back for all my recent borrowing. Plus the bar was the only place in town where they still knew me, and I hoped he might see that I was popular in certain circles.

"Minky!" I shouted.

She gave Riley one of her nicer smiles. It occurred to me that he could practice with Mink before taking a stab at Pine—get rid of the virgin stigma—but this was a nasty thought, made nastier by the thought of Meli's little face and by the fact that Riley was hiccupping fiercely.

"You haven't even had a *drink* yet," I said.

He shrugged.

"Been a while since I've seen you," said Mink. "How are you?"

"Good," Riley said, not looking up.

I elbowed him.

"How are you?" he added.

We took our glasses to a booth. I rubbed the inside of my wrist, scratched my elbow, and felt my brother wishing that I'd worn something more than an undershirt. He didn't like looking at my shoulder. The sailor's ghost had a crooked face; the dragon was pretty, but how his tail went into the doll's mouth was disturbing; and the doll, cherries for eyes, looked dead. Though the stars were hidden, Riley saw them. Leaden circles printed on the skin. When he'd found me in the basement pushing a cigarette into my shoulder, he hadn't called out. My burning skin had smelled horse-mouth gray. I threw the butt at the cinder-block wall, wiped my eyes with the back of my hand, then noticed Riley standing there. Don't tell, I'd said.

"Something wrong with your beer?"

"It's fine," he said, "I'm just drinking it slowly."

"So how's work and all?"

"It's fine."

In a family of overtalkers, how had he ended up this way? I stifled a yawn. "Fine as in you love it, or fine as in it's okay for the next six months until you find a better job?"

"Fine as in I don't love it but don't want to apply somewhere else either."

"Ah so," I said, glancing across at Mink, who had not come over to chat as she normally would on a slow early Tuesday. *Please come over to chat.*

Riley was saying my name. I snapped back to attention.

"What's that?"

"I need to go home."

"'Tis but nine forty-five! I'll fetch us another round."

"I have a job," he said.

"Good for you. Beer again, or something else?"

"Neither."

Life of the party, this one. "Well, fine, let me just see if there's anyone I need to say goodbye to…" I stood and surveyed the room; surely an associate or two was here. Surely.

THE MAIN CHARACTER in the book we had to write a paper on was obsessed with his sister, kept thinking of her while he got ready to drown himself. The sister wasn't dead as far as I could tell, but the book was confusing; she might be dead. Or was she just a slut? Dead to the family on account of sluttery? I consulted the blank notebook page, hoping I might already have jotted something down, and looked again at Nzambi's list of essay topics. *1) How does the novel's narrative structure engage questions of time and memory?* I wrote in the notebook: *This paper is even more retarded than the retarded brother character.* I was in my underwear, but it was starting to get very warm in the room, unbreathable. The cone of desk-lamp light was burning all the oxygen; my chest ached. If I had to escape, there was the bed in my way, and the other chair, and the mountain of clothes Mert said was evidence of a disorganized mind. *It is Tuesday night you're in your room in your house but my voice got sucked away.* My eyes were blurrying. The light had scorched up all the air. I staggered to the window and groped at the sash, which wouldn't rise; I squatted for leverage, then fell over. *2) How does the sister's absence act as a presence?* The blurried eyes were worsening. I couldn't hear my own voice. Not a single crumb of air was left in the room. The next thing was my cheek pushed into the carpet and my eyes level with a dust bunny. I sat up wet-skinned. When I was able to stand I went to the mirror and was impressed by how white my face had gone. I was so damn pale already, who knew I could get whiter? I'd passed out, which was kind of interesting—more interesting, certainly, than the retarded paper I was not going to write.

"Don't call me bitch." My sister shoved herself to the edge. Her shoulder poked up.

"I didn't," I said.

She was waiting.

Finally: "Sorry."

The shoulder lowered. She turned her face to me in the hot dark and said, "Yeah you should be." Giggled. "I *so* can't sleep. How are you s'posed to sleep when it's like a steaming *washcloth* is over you?"

I grabbed at the soft part above her elbow. "So will you switch places now?"

She said okay, but only this one time.

We crawled over each other, switching. I liked her side better because it was closer to the wall.

Her eyelids were shaking. I watched them lower. "No school tomorrow," she said in a small contented voice.

I yawned: "You're a genius detective."

"True," she said, smiling with her eyes shut.

We had deep-dish pizza the night after she died. Somebody brought over two larges, hamburger and plain. The curly nubs of burger were her flesh except cooked and good-smelling, so I did not eat. Riley ate a shit ton, then puked in the downstairs bathroom.

I THRASHED IN night waves until three octopi saved me. They dragged me to the horizon. Green foam drank me. Through black sky jumped a long-haired star. I would never know land again. Then the boy and the curtain. Tall red pleats. I was naked. He was naked. Red lines ran down his white skin. He wanted to. I wanted to. *Am I allowed? You never got to.* But it was happening: he was in me. He was too big for—

Radio. National publicky voice. *Thirty-nine prisoners,* it said, *have died in U.S. custody in Iraq and Afghanistan since the fall of 2001 and there have been ninety-four cases of proven or suspected abuse, according to a new report by the army.*

Orange bash of hammer on black-draped human skull. Fake-bloody white fingers scraping brown cheek—

I clicked it off and sat up into another day of unemployment. It still felt strange to imagine not being greeted, five times a week, by that grummy stucco square. I needed to ask my parents for a tide-over. Oh Cadmus, what shall become of me?

Scrape, scrape. Shut up, I said to the wall. Fucker must have been huge by now, living off the land-fat—maple icing, canned cheese—huge, and diseased, and dead the second he showed his face. The hammer awaited! I'd been wondering if the rat chewed me in the night. Now and again along my forearms, between my ribs, was a red dent I couldn't account for. What size *precisely* was a rat mouth? Tiny rustlings: I slammed my elbow at the dry-wall, pain welcome, all blood dashing to that spot. Sun. Hot. Hurts. Ankles cracking on the way to the toilet. Dark yellow piss—sign of illness? Insurance was one thing I hadn't lost, because the bookstore had never provided it. The bathroom sill was a tiny museum: air plant growing from a coral ball, splinter of blue glass, Cam's pomade jar, the beer tab he'd given me one day after class. You can wear it like this, he'd said and slid it onto my pinky and for the rest of the day it had been like being his wife, even if he'd picked the wrong finger. That was before we'd ever even kissed, yet I felt married. Being fifteen in honors English—those days were petals, safe and whole, unhurt.

I jogged to the kitchen, returned with the hammer in both hands. Swung back like in baseball and the hammer met the wall; plaster sprayed into my mouth. I'd tidy it up later. First water in the kettle, bread in the oven. Fuckedly, I was out of butter. Cherry jelly on the knife, smooth; I'd only buy it if no lumps of fruit meat were visible through the jar glass. Poured water across the coffee, waited for it to trickle, brought cup and plate to the floor by the couch and punched on the game. This one was called Cull and the object was simple: kill every citizen over thirty. You had a range of devices at your disposal—gun, sword, nunchucks, gilded mirror. You roamed the high street at dusk, when folks were flocking into public houses; picked out the thinning hairdos, the broadening flanks. Using your silencer, you delivered a bullet into a brain. A forty-two-year-old dropped softly to the pavement; nobody minded. A pack of guilloteens surrounded an injured thirty-five-year-old, cackling at its pain until one teen chopped its throat with an ax. Good riddance! sang a naked-except-for-stilettos boy who sank a heel into the dead old back.

Go on, pick up the receiver.

I pulled it off the cradle, dialed, put it back down.

Again up, again dial.

"Good morning," said my mother.

"Good morning," I said.

"How are things?"

"Great, you?"

"Oh, we're fine—"

"So Mert!"

"Mmm?"

"Question for you."

"Fire away."

I coughed. "Well, I need to ask you a favor."

"Oh?"

"So, just, the bookstore closing is kind of taking its toll cash-wise, and I was just wondering if I could get a loan—I mean I'll probably find something this week, but I won't have my first paycheck for at least two—"

"What sort of a loan?" she said, not in a nice way.

"Well, rent money for this month and also utilities, I guess?"

No response.

"Mert?"

"I'm here."

"So…" My face was horribly hot.

"Quinn, if you are repeatedly unable to meet your financial obligations, you need to take a serious look at your lifestyle and make changes accordingly. Your father and I cannot, simply *can*not keep bailing you out."

"I know, it's just—"

"Just what? Even when you *had* a job you couldn't always pay your bills. Which is difficult to understand, frankly."

"Okay, I get it. Thanks anyway. See you soon, Mert."

"Hold on a—"

I hung up.

With electrical tape I patched the hole, although little chance in hell remained of getting back my security deposit. Landlord: *You leaving food on the floor? Vermin come when people are filthy.* I stuck the tape on gently, lest the drywall collapse further. The point was to deny the rat such an obvious portal. Force him to use ingenuity.

A GIRL HAD said it stopped your period. This girl's older sister used to not eat and she never got her period ever. So how long would the sister go without food? Days, probably. Or she'd eat an apple and a carrot and that was it. And lots of water. Water is *crucial.* The gym teacher yelled at us to get back to layups. "Deliver the ball *gently* to the rim," he shouted, "as if you were giving a gift!"

She never got her period ever.

And all it took was not eating? I laughed out loud.

I quit the sandwiches and started going to lunch in the cafeteria, where I drank no-sugar iced tea and chewed on hard noodles from the salad bar.

THREE DAYS SINCE I sent the letter. The letter had been short. I did not catch Cam up on my life, merely wrote I'd heard he was in town and wanted to know how he was doing. That I hoped he was well.

DON'T BE SCARED *it's not bad it's good.* She worried about pimples, but not about the shapes and scents flying around in our heads. We got born lucky, she believed, able to see things in a way other people couldn't. But I did not want to see them that way. I wanted to be regular, like Riley, who hated when we talked about what color a number was, or a sound. Jealous, my sister reminded me, but I was jealous too—of Riley's clean brain that took in noises as plain noises, names as plain names instead of boxes of sensation. *Smell of trees. Darkest green.* At school, at first, they thought I was slow. *Nine minus two is purple and a boy.* Colors were the only way I could talk about numbers. It sounded wrong when I said it out loud, but it made total sense in my head—in there, never a mess. Girls, look at this room. What a goddamn mess. These (Mert snatched dresses from the floor) need to be hung up. And these (grabbing shirts thrown over a chair back) should be folded, not slopped! When your room's all ahoo, she added, it makes your mind disorganized.

My sister laughed and said, I prove your theory wrong
because my room is messy but my mind is *very* orga-
nized. Stop showing off, said our mother, it's not becoming. I'm just saying, she said but smaller.

Cam wanted to know why I hadn't heard the gunshot.
How come I didn't wake up until morning.
    I just didn't, I told him.
    But my parents? My brother?
    We'd all slept all night.

RILEY'S KITCHEN WAS idiotically clean, as his whole apartment tended to be: every surface flashing from a recent swipe, not a speck or crumb in sight. I left my juice glass on the counter and counted the number of seconds—six—it took him to remove it to the sink, soap, rinse, and rack it.

"How've you been?"

"Fine, how are you?"

"I'm good!" I say. "Hey do you want to get some dinner?"

"No thanks. I had a big, um, snack."

"You sure? What about some Ethiopian?"

"I'm not hungry," Riley said. He reached for the chain on my collarbone. "You haven't worn this in a long time. Where's it from, again?"

"Cam's bike. He wrecked it in the park." I backed away, took the links in my own fingers. "Do you remember our video for 'Safety-Pin Improvisation in the Wilderness'? I was wearing this, remember? The director had that wandering eye that slid around all over the place—"

Riley, nodding, made a room in his head: quick, thick, soft-walled. He had heard it all before.

"So no dinner?"

"Sorry," he said, "I'm just not—"

"Hungry. Right. Okay, then, well—oh, I have something to ask you, almost forgot!"

His eyes went smaller. Who could blame him.

"So...huh, this is a weird request kind of, but...I have to move out of my apartment next month, and..."

"How come?"

"They're selling the building to developers."

"Oh really," he said.

"So I was wondering if I could crash here for a week, couple of weeks, just until I get a new place?"

"More space at Mert and Fod's," he pointed out.

"Yeah, but Mert and Fod are there."

"Well—"

"Oh thank you, Coyote—"

He sighed. "Only for a little while."

I SAT UP in the covers, listening: the clomp of heavier shoes than Fod wore, and a chair being moved, and Mert's fluttery feet going to the kitchen, where she opened the icebox with more gusto than usual. Where was my brother? I didn't want to go down alone.

"Ri?" I pounded the wall.

"I know," he called back.

"*Quinn*! Riley!" Her voice was angry, though an outsider wouldn't have been able to tell. Only the family could hear the tiny knots that grew on our mother's vocal cords.

Riley was standing outside my door when I opened it. "Were you napping?" he said.

"Yeah," I said. "It's cold today."

"Yeah," he said, although cold wasn't why we napped.

"Oh children," Mert said downstairs, "look who's here."

Mr. Walker got clumsily up from the armchair, bald head popping with sweat, big red hands sticking out of checked sleeves. "Hello," he said.

He's scared fuckless, I thought, and he should be. He should be frightened for the rest of his life.

"Hello," Riley said and shook the red hand.

I folded my arms.

"Well!" huffed Walker, sitting back down, "it's good to see you two."

Shouldn't be two, should be *three,* you gun-loving fuckface. I should slice your throat but my knife's upstairs.

"I'm making tea," announced our mother. "Some nice hot tea on a winter's day." She didn't normally sound like a detergent commercial.

"That sounds nice," agreed Walker.

Riley glared at the carpet, off somewhere, not with us. I kicked him gently to drag him back; I needed an ally. His little sock twitched.

"How are your new schools?" bellowed Walker.

"They're just fine," Mert said. "Some excellent teachers."

"Our school system," I said loudly, "is ranked forty-sixth in the nation, but at least we're beating Mississippi."

The kettle shrieked and Mert said, "Excuse me."

We excused her and sat, Walker and the two who should have been three, in silence. "You know, kids," he said eventually and I braced for it *please don't please don't please don't* but Walker did not. He covered his mouth with hammy fingers and stayed that way until our mother brought in a tray of blue and white tea equipment we had never seen before.

Later, Riley twisted a licorice strand around his finger and sucked it and asked, "Where did those cups come from?"

"She probably bought them special," I said, "for the gun-loving fuckface."

"But she didn't know he was coming over—maybe they were from her bridal drowsy," Riley said. He placed a red coil on my knee. I nudged it off onto his bed and he yelped: "No food on the bed! Ants will come!" and I said, "Stupid, it's *winter*, the ants are all sleeping."

"IF LOST DEEP in the California wild, how would you stay alive?"

"Suckle honey," said the youngest.

"Carve a bow and arrow to slay animals," said the oldest, who was playing again even though she had quit the game, for good, many times.

The middle had devised the question to showcase her own superior reply: "I would find a buckeye tree and gather its deadly nuts, which Native Americans used to put in rivers to make fish sleepy. The river dilutes the poison from the nut so the fish don't die, they're only sort of stunned, and you can scoop them right out of the water."

It was a thing the youngest and the oldest couldn't stand about the middle: her need to be smarter than they were.

EVEN THOUGH WE'D been told it was not going to be a free-for-all, I turned on the television at every opportunity. Riley did too, since it hid other noises, like Mert's crying; but we were always aware that if we pushed our luck, the machine would be taken away.

"It's morning again in America!" it said cheerfully. "Today, more men and women will go to work than ever before in our country's history. With interest rates and inflation down, more people are buying new homes, and our new families can have confidence in the future—"

"For god's sake shut *up!*" Mert yelled from the kitchen.

"But I wasn't—"

"Not *you*, pettle, that bastard's reelection ad."

"America today is prouder and stronger and better," continued the ad. "Why would we want to return to where it was less than four short years ago?"

IT WAS WARM enough that today I would have something to talk about at the convenience store, could say, Did you know this city was built on a swamp? and wait for Two Thumbs to say yeah he knew. Up at the counter I took my customary peek at the baby tentacle, and was stunned to see the hand—the whole hand—bundled in white gauze. Had there been a surgery? Had the tentacle been *chopped*? But why would he have wanted to do that? The nub brought him luck! The guy was calm as ever, ringing up purchases with the good hand, while I could barely get out Hello.

The radio on a shelf above the register reported how many American soldiers had died last month.

The man in line behind me said, "Goddamn ridiculous."

Two Thumbs said, "Right?" and slid me a pack.

The man added, "My sister's boy is over there."

My apartment was even sweltier than outdoors. The fate of the tentacle troubled me—had wrecked the morning—made me unable, in fact, to look through the want ads. *The male knows nothing of the beauty he's hacked off a limb for and the female knows of her mate only the fertilizing arm.* Maybe Two Thumbs had cut away his limb to impregnate someone. Stuffed the bloody nub up a girl's causeway, left it lodged there until it sprouted?

I glanced again at my answering machine, but no red light. It had now been a full week since Cam should've gotten my note. A week meant the person wasn't going to call or write back. A week was not covered by any of the usual excuses.

I ripped open the new deck. Where were the matches hiding.

The only thing I could think of was to go to bed again. It was eleven fifteen in the morning. I finished the cigarette and tacked the zebra sheet back up across the window. Beeps and whistles batted soft at the eardrum, and I watched their tinfoil twinings as I dropped toward sleep. Dreamt of nurses in an Arctic hospital, naked but for white caps and, at their necks, white stoles.

AT MY FRIEND'S house, in a room walled by windows, it was too loud, too much window. I put my hands on my eyes against the nickel of Sunday-morning light. Observatory Place had drapes, but this modern fancy kind of house didn't. My friend—Julie? Janie? Janice? Janine?—slept on. I hated waking before the other person; the only thing to do was get a book from the shelf, and I wasn't the biggest reader. Finally she got up and we headed for the kitchen, hoping for doughnuts; instead, before we'd even finished the stairs, I smelled pancakes. Thick black blood. I started to throw up but swallowed it.

"Good morning, ladies," said my friend's mother. "These are hot off the griddle!"

"Yum," my friend said. She got the juice. I breathed through my teeth, heart batting. Juice didn't help, only made my mouth sweeter and the blood blacker, swelling in the air, it slid down the walls of the air and I could smell my sister's body—

"Here you go," the mother said and put a plate before me.

"No thank you." I expected the mother to remove the plate, but it stayed.

The mother's tongue went clock-clock. "Why don't you try a *little*," she said.

I could barely breathe. "They look good but no thank you."

"Are you allergic?" she suggested.

"No I just don't eat them."

"Oh, well, that's a little rigid, don't you think? You're much too thin, you know—"

"Mom shut *up*," said my friend.

"I'm sorry if I say what I think, dear, but it's obvious how skinny she's gotten. Why don't you try *one* pancake—they're not too big."

"I can't eat pancakes!" I shouted.

My friend whined, "Jesus, Mom, way to go."

The more I cried, the hotter and blacker went the smell, tarring my chest, drowning every lung hair. My sister's name was filling my mouth, wanting to be said, pushing into a scream; but I couldn't unclench my teeth.

"I think she needs to go home," the mother said. "I'll call her mother."

"That woman thinks you're anorexic." Mert stared at the road, her hands on the wheel at ten and two.

"Well I'm not."

"That's what I told her, of course—and incidentally I have no idea why she thinks she can make a diagnosis like that—but she said as soon as those pancakes were on the table, you acted, quote, like a horse who'd seen a snake."

"Well I'm fine, so can we stop talking about it?"

We drove for a while. The rain was louder than our breathing. Then, almost home: "But why did you react that way to the pancakes? I'm just curious, pettle."

"I didn't feel like eating them and she kept being pushy even when I told her no thank you."

"She can certainly be pushy," Mert nodded. "I've seen her at parent–teacher meetings."

MY LEGS WERE taking me to the subway, but my head could not supply a destination post that. Well, air-conditioning would be enough. I'd sit on the cool train awhile, unsteaming my synapses. One day soon, when I was completely deaf and not just vaguely hard of hearing, I could be a trainy, one of those people who just rode, in winter and summer, to stay out of the weather. I would still have my eyes, which could look out, once the red line came up out of the ground, at the gray fields of suburb.

From the black of the tunnel I knew it was there above me, my city, tight side streets and soil in squares for trees to come up from and the broad paved spokes running from the circles and the streets after rain with that itchy wet smell, a hard fog rising and gone, and the streets after snow with brown hills crusting and the streets after protests dotted with napkins and bottles and flags. I got homesick for Edinburgh Lane but only the version I'd made up later, good parts bigger, bad parts gone. My sister was a fish, floppy and bleeding, needing ice, fish pie, a fish-eyed stiff. In twenty years a body could do a lot of crumbling. Coyote and I could have visited the graveyard in darkness, with shovels, to check how much meat had come off the bones. By now she must have been so dry even the worms weren't interested.

When the train got tiresome I went to the bar. From the way Mink's eyes were shining, I knew bad news was afoot.

"Our friend is not doing so hot," she whispered.

I looked around. Saw no friends.

Pinching my elbow: "*Geck.* In here yesterday all loaded. Just booze, I think—but still."

"The nidget didn't even get to ninety this time, did he?"

"I don't count his days for him," she huffed. "And if he's drinking now, he'll be on dodge soon enough. I don't know how he keeps coming up with the *cash.* He's not even working. How could he possibly fund it?"

"Petty crime," I suggested.

"But he's too stupid for crime."

From the bar pay phone I called Ajax, who answered hissing: "It's one forty-five in the fucking morning."

"But are you up?"

"No," he said. "What's wrong?"

"Nothing," I said. "Just wanted to see how you were doing, you know, with the bookstore sadness and—"

"I'm fine," he snapped. "Good night."

He hadn't cared that I didn't have a college degree, or that I didn't read much. He had seen us play a bunch of times and he told me, during our interview, "You guys wrote fantastic songs." *Geck wrote the fantastic ones,* I did not say. Ajax was fingering some huge dark beads around his neck. "Hard, what happened," he added, meaning the accident that ended the band, but I thought, at first, he meant my sister—thought *How could you know about that?*—and my eyes prickled hard. Maybe he only hired me because he had brought me to tears.

RILEY HANDED ME a papier-mâché face. In sixth-grade art they were doing Halloween masks.

"Nice," I said and handed it back.

"No, it's for you."

I fingered its glitter crust. "Thanks but I'm not, like, gonna *wear* it."

Our father's car was out front and when we climbed to the porch we heard Mert screaming inside. Not screaming—choking? We heard: "Oh God oh God oh God."

"It's okay," I said and rested my palm on Riley's head. Before I could finish unlocking the door, Fod opened it.

"Kids, your mother's having a rough day. Go on up to the park."

"For how long?" I asked.

"Just go."

The choke-squalls were worse with the door open. "Is she okay?"

"She'll be fine—now go."

We went. I steered us to a picnic table and Riley opened his backpack to see which library books he had and I lit a cigarette. Smoked half, heeled it out, lit another.

"Here," said Riley, and gave me a snail that he kept in a secret pocket of the backpack.

I made Riley sit at the picnic table as long as possible, afraid of finding, at home, exactly what we found: her still coughing and weeping. It smelled of onions frying; Fod was in the kitchen to escape her. She was balled up in a chair, forehead on elbow, shaking her head.

"Mert are you okay?"

"No, squid, I'm not."

I wished she would just fake it.

"Should we go back to the park?" asked Riley, looking up at me with such trust that I spat, "Fuck no." He shouldn't have trusted me. "Fod?" I called through the onion. "Are we eating soon?"

"Yep!" he shouted back. "Want to set the table?"

MY BROTHER AND I packed what I owned. The weather had turned cold again, but I was drenched—muscles tiny from lack of use, heart stiff from smoking. Riley busied himself with the silverware and cups while I slid armfuls of records into boxes, singing nonsense.

"You still have a good voice," called my brother.

"Shucks," I said.

He sized up the kitchen table. In its drawer were my million rubber bands.

"Do you pick out a new one every *day*?"

"Depends," I said.

"But some days you don't wear one—how do you decide?"

How had such an earnest person managed to land in our family? I told him that I gauged my daily panic level the minute after waking.

"Do you want to keep these takeout menus?"

"Why the fuck would I?"

"Oh. I don't—okay." They went into the trash bag; his cheeks flared.

"Sorry, Coyote, you're totally helping out and I'm being a . . . "

"It's all right."

I came to squat over the pile of newspapers in the corner. Underneath were the posters and pages, the yellow photographs—

"What is all that?"

"Documentation of fecal matter," I explained. "Which I wanted to torch but couldn't figure out where." Into the trash bag they went.

He was staring at my calf, which had a sea-green vein he'd never noticed before. Well on its way to being the leg of an elderly.

"I think my familiar has left the building," I offered.

"The rat, you mean?"

I nodded. "No more thumpings in the night. Haven't heard him in two days. He must have smelled the packing and known cleaning fluids would follow in its wake." I added a laugh, for Riley's sake, but actually I was a little bothered that I had not gotten to say goodbye to the creature. Or kill it.

The radio told how bad the traffic was getting on the bridges. It did not talk about the female soldiers or their periody underwear. The blood was food coloring stirred into water, but the prisoners didn't know this. They believed the red was real.

WHEN I GREW stars on my shoulder, nobody saw them at first. I started growing them spring of tenth grade, about the time I picked up smoking and discovered a band I loved more than any I had yet heard. The sounds this band made were torn wings, crusts of glitter hills, valleys of black flame, clouds cut in three by red lightning, bluish brain rising from cankered feet. Every hair on me pointed at the ceiling. The thick poles of sadness that stood in me were yanked out by the singer's screeching and howling, and my shoulders fluttered. The drums were heaving and keeling and thwacking, each hit pulling the veins in my chest closer to the surface. The people onstage didn't look any older than we were, white boys on whose fatless bodies hung cotton and denim, nothing especially special—but they *knew* something. They were pilots of the new land, beckoning *Over here, over here!* and I felt superior to every other kid in the room because I alone (I believed) was having my veins brought to the surface.

The magicians played again the following week after a protest at the university. I didn't care about South Africa but Cam made me go; it was important, he said, horrible things were happening and we had to do something. Horrible things, I thought, have already happened. But I queued up with the rest of them, a line of kids in black britches and gray glimmies, scarred boots and leathers, hair chopped up. They yelled, Divest! and End apart-hate now!—pale cheeks tomato-ing with righteous anger and June heat. I did not yell; I was merely waiting for that night's show.

Apartheid No, Freedom Yes! they screamed in the bar. Practically every kid in there had also been at the protest. Cam screamed too. A guy from our English class bought us whiskeys with his brother's license. With each sip, I brightened. I could not wait for my new loves to take the stage. Cam kept brushing against me. I brushed back. "I bet your hand is smaller than mine," he babbled, holding his palm up. I pressed mine to it. "Shit, a whole knuckle smaller." We kept our hands like that for a long time, and when he looked at me, I did not look away.

In his parents' car, after, he stared at the wheel, a true smile on his mouth. Then he turned. "Um, hey."

"Yeah?"

"Come here," he said.

Our mouths bumped; I smelled whiskey; his lips were dry, at first.

BECAUSE RILEY'S BUILDING didn't have mailboxes, the postman threw everything onto the hall radiator, and you had to sort. I saw flickers of the lives going on in other apartments. Man on the ground: antiwar pamphlets, amateur magician newsletter. Woman on the fourth: hand-stitched brocade envelopes from an unpronounceable town in Wales—faraway lover, or devoted aunt?

Nothing from Cam, of course. Maybe he never even got my letter. What if the secretary had misspelled the address? Or what if he'd called my apartment after I moved out? *You left a forwarding notice.* But what if the phone company had mixed up two digits of Riley's number?

My brother's mail was a postcard inviting him to attend a furniture sale. His name on the label was a blue cube, and salty. No flavor if someone spoke it, only when I saw it written down. My own name written was chewed aluminum foil: sore, bright, silver-black.

If the Russian writer whose numbers had colors and feelings had been a genius, then maybe we sisters were too. I said doubtfully, "Genius?" and my sister said, "We *could* be. Mert and Fod should've put us in a *special school.*" She made me bring my library books to the basement, where we would read for an hour before dinner to sharpen our brains; and she reminded me not to tell Riley. He would feel bad, she explained, for not being a genius too.

But the fact was, I was just as normal-brained as Riley, except I heard colors. Only our sister had any genius in her.

From the windows upstairs I couldn't see the door to Mrs. Jones's parlor, only the people using it. Here, a big-bubbed college student; there, a crew-cutted soldier. 8:52 PM: handholding couple with matching white veins in their ears—the girl's idea to go, I was guessing, and the boy humoring her. Mrs. Jones stayed open until midnight on weekends because people were more likely to buy fortunes when drunk.

The bathroom had no windows and was big enough for a little table where Riley had laid out pans and strung up a wire. In his pans floated smoky prints, harsh and cold. He would have stayed in here forever, safe from people, if he hadn't worried that the chemicals would eat tunnels in his skin. He played no music here. All was flat: the sheets of silver paper, the taut wire clipped with drenched images, water dripping neatly into the pans.

In the crowd of icebox pictures, Cam laughed on the steep cracked steps of Belfry Street, and barrettes had caught the black spilling hair so you could see his eyes, and his cheeks were dark from not shaving. Riley had taken this one himself—had told Cam not to smile, which was a good way to get a person to smile.

The spider-haired girl from the video channel, throwing out minor questions at the interview's end: "So what about you and the drummer? You have an obvious rapport onstage—and you're the two founding members—ever any romantics between you?"

Me: "We tried that on for size in high school, but…"

What was I, a vacuum-cleaner salesman? *Tried that on for size.* There were things you wished you could suck back into your mouth.

RILEY GROPED ALONG the rough plaster for the switch. The basement scared him. Our sister's boxes were down there. He couldn't find the light—oh, there. The bulb flickered. He stepped very quietly, waiting at each wooden step. Heard grunts. And me crying. The sobs came in little shots. Someone was hurting me? Faster grunting. It took him a while of listening to figure out the other voice was Cam's, and that I was not being hurt, or not exactly.

We had sex twelve days after the kiss in his parents' car. Neither of us had done it before. Embarrassed to be a virgin still at sixteen, I pretended, at first, to know what I was doing; but it was Cam, hard to lie to. Plus I was afraid I'd bleed. In Nzambi's class we had read the old classic psychology treatise about a girl who left a red mark on the sheet and was frantic to change it so the family maid wouldn't see evidence of her sluttiness. Most manuals warn of first-time blood. What if I leaked enough for the worm to smell it, smile on its eyeless face, and start crawling at me? Towel, I thought. I could be quick, mop up before the smell traveled.

"What are you doing?" Cam asked when I got onto my knees and stared at the rug.

"Checking something," I said.

BELLS, CRAZY BELLS, bumpy under me: what? Oh yes. How'd you get *there*, octopus?

Dots of pain flew at my eyes. I would sew it back on—but I couldn't sew—get my mother to sew it—but she couldn't sew—she was a failure, she always said, as a housewife—and my father didn't sew because men didn't—so Octy was crippled forever, and I hated my sister. It was only a stupid *game*! Why should I keep on playing a game that was so giantly stupid, named after people dead a million years, during which I was obliged to do giantly boring things like hold the end of the sheet while my sister wrap-twirled into a mummy?

She had taken a knife to Octy.

I rubbed my eyes, pressed the pain in deeper. I was too old to cry. I hated being oldest. My sister's crime would not be punished enough. In my wet fingers I held the amputated tentacle, tufted at its broken end, bloodless.

As the oldest, you got in trouble the most and for things you hadn't even done. *Where did all the ice cream go? Riley. What? Riley ate it. Why the hell did you let him do that?* The little ones were smaller, which made them cuter and less hittable. Fod used to hit us all, but me the hardest. As I grew, I measured my height compulsively, recording each new quarter inch on the door frame, believing that if I got taller than my father, he would be afraid to touch me.

After my sister died, he stopped hitting. It was one of the perks.

I was never up early; but the tidiness of Riley's apartment disturbed sleep. The white walls were so loud. He had a proper toaster, which I loved, no waiting for an oven to heat; and he bought new bread from a real bakery, God bless him. I noticed his crumby morning plate and decided to wash it so he would mind my presence less.

The world looked astoundingly clean at this hour. Everywhere was the strumming of quicker blood, a clicking of the day's gears; across every building (none more than ten stories) the new pink sun laid a stripe; water clung in beads to grass blades and parking meters, soon to die in the heat and therefore brave; and the people were emerging with their game faces on. The gainfully employed marched past: ironed-flat normals, spruce girls with calamity cuts. My hair was an old brown hang. I inhaled fresh shampoo from pedestrian necks, little glows that would be gone by midmorning. Bog-sweat hadn't yet ruined the air, but it would, any day now, I was bracing myself. So humid your shoes went green inside. The pedestrian current swelled as the bells fell down the hill. Out of the current, the city rested—here, a stone ledge clean of pigeons; there, a red stoop—but inside it, all was rushing.

Here was the doughnut shop. *A maple, ma'am? Why thank you, I think I just might!* Teeth sank happily into sugar-bright flesh. *A second maple, methinks.* The shop was blessedly noisy, hot with machines and voices and traffic to conceal the beeps. Legally deaf by forty was my prediction. If correct, I'd buy a state-of-the-art gaming system (including projector and wireless controls) with my disability check. And I wouldn't be able to hear Mert tell me, ever again, that it wasn't much of a life.

At 10:04 I sallied down the block to the chain store. I would enter with confidence, chin high. With any luck, the manager would be a local and old enough to know me. Pastel carpet, blond shelves, disinfected air. I mourned the smoke-friendly dinge of our dead store. Gave my cockiest grin to the infant behind the counter, who forgot to smile back.

"Help you?"

"Yeah, I'm wondering if you guys are hiring?"

I waited for a bloom of recognition *OhmyGod is that—?* on the hairless cheeks.

"Sorry, man. We've been slow. The Web is fucking us all in the A."

"Who's the manager here?"

But the infant said a name I didn't know.

HOW LONG DID you have to not eat before it quit coming for good? I wanted so badly to eat bread again, chocolate and butter and sugar again, but the books did not tell me when I might. I hadn't bled in four months, which was not long enough, probably, to ensure everlasting drought.

I asked the school librarian if there were any more detailed medical encyclopedias.

A girl stopped me at the lockers: "Can I ask you something?" She was a popular girl and I had never spoken to her. "Um, a few of us have been wondering—is there something—are you, like, *taking* anything?"

I frowned.

"Because you look fabulous. Are you taking something?"

"No," I said.

The girl said, "Then how are you getting the weight off?"

I said, "I'm not doing anything."

"Yes you are," hissed the girl.

I shook my head.

"Whatever," the girl snorted.

And Riley said at home: "When did you get so hairy?"

"I'm not."

"Yes you *are!*" He ran two fingers along my arm. "Look at that fuzz. You're *fuzzy.*"

"I am not," I said at the back of my mouth.

"Fod she looks like a cat!"

"There's nothing wrong with her," Fod said. "She's going through puberty, there's naturally some extra hair growth…"

"But Fod she's like a skeleton with fur."

I could barely breathe my heart was going so hard. They would take me to a doctor, who'd give me pills to force the blood to grow. And back the worm would come.

38 DOLLARS LAST night. This is exactly why we are going to take the Offer, no matter what says Cameron the Virtuous. Less than 40 American bills. Guy hands it to me and I'm like OK, still waiting, and he goes That's it man sorry slow night. One days worth of gas and tobacco. Slow night he says, like we were the polka unit at Penis Oaks Retirement Village. We are taking the Offer.

ON THE PORCH I propped myself like a Southern gentleman of yore, boots on railing, hand closed around beading glass of liquor—no mint, but it could have loosely been classified as a julep. "Are you crazy?" I inquired of the cardinal on a low branch brushing near. Bird stared back. "Are you?" louder, and bird jumped away. Watching its flittery progress down Observatory Place, I noticed a guy standing—just standing, not doing a single thing—across the street. He wore a sort of cape. He was perhaps one of those creatures who dressed as their favorite fantasy character when the movie came out but forgot to take off the costume. What the dickens was he doing? His face, if he had one, was hidden by hood and noonday glare.

I sat up with difficulty and called: "Hey!"

Capey moved not.

"Be warned, I'm in the neighborhood watch…"

Now he moved. Down the street. At a brisk clip.

If Mert had been around, I would have informed her that the area, once a bourgeois stronghold, was getting sketchy. But she and Fod were on campus, slaving away while their middle-aged daughter lolled on their front porch to escape the apartment of their not-quite-middle-aged son. This street was plagued by sketchy capes, but pretty too—trees all bursting green, and little red flowers at the fences. The paper lay open at the want ads. Just look on the computer, Riley had said. But I preferred the feel of a newspaper. I liked how the print stained my fingers, proof of effort, and how a newspaper made me appear, to passersby, just another citizen—an American taxpayer who knew how to fill a day properly, with a job and lunch at restaurants and kisses for her husband upon returning to her toy-strewn castle moated by lemon trees. *And where's my dear offspring I am never not nice to?*—the offspring running qualmless into her arms.

The morning lumbered on without any reappearance from the cape wearer. I made my way through an entire can of chips to defray the effects of the almost-julep. At 1:00 PM I would get up from the porch and become relevant. I would enjob myself, somehow. Riley needed not fear: I would be gone from his couch before he could realize how very much he would miss me.

LAST NIGHT WAS *town of sickified kids, really worst kind of kid, bred in suburbs but wild to catch plague of streets. Shitlings couldn't be bothered to clap—after every song it was like somebody died—then vampirina put a shriveled rose on the stage at G's feet which was the cherry on that crapcake and I said into the mic Where's my rose? and this bunch of girls screams You don't get one! and then, worst and worser, was looking down at the bunch of girls and one's face was exactly like hers—I mean exactly—hair not same but face a replica, tiny ghost staring up at me and I couldn't member how to start Northern Direction. G had to play the intro 5x. The ghost nodded along but didn't clap.*

NO MATTER HOW hard I clenched my eyes, I still saw the sound her voice made, a forest branch, a green so black it could barely be heard.

Why are you here?

To talk to you.

But I don't want to.

Yes you do, I know you miss me.

No I don't.

Yes you do, Quinn.

No.

Don't lie, it's not becoming. Now let me back in, okay?

But I can't.

If you try hard enough, you can.

But I've tried really hard and I can't figure out how!

You haven't tried your hardest. Better hurry, because the worm is coming.

I don't know how to!

Well figure out fast, because listen, the worm—do you hear him sniffing?

She could smell in a forest if a wolfberry grew.

Something was on my arm. Patting.

    A voice: "You were shouting."

    I sat up.

    "You were shouting in your sleep," Riley said.

    I watched him go—now back—a glass of water.

    "Thanks, Coyote." I sipped.

    "Better?"

    "Yes."

    I held my lips tight so the worm could not glide out. For a long time the worm had been gone and I ate whatever I wanted. Cam had brought it back.

"BODY LANGUAGE," SAID the group leader, "is very important in communication!"

The room stank of old hamburger, which was brutal in a room of people afraid of food. Even the overeaters were afraid. "Body language!" the leader repeated. "Think about it—it says everything! I'm closed; I'm open; I'm wary; I'm interested; I'm not paying attention!" She paused in her pacing around the chair circle to clear her mucousy throat. It made me nervous to have her walk behind us. Why was she outside the circle? Weren't we *in this together* as she often proclaimed?

I could feel my mother thinking it was all quite ridiculous. She sat still, one leg neatly over the other, hands clasped on her thigh, and her face was polite but behind it, I knew—

"Crossing one's legs, for instance!" the leader cried. "What does that say about one's attitude? It says: I'm guarding myself! I am not open to new ideas! But if both feet are on the floor—now that's a different message!

Uncrossed legs say: I am willing to consider new ideas! I am not shutting myself off—no, in fact, I'm *listening*!"

My fingers tore a strip of notebook paper smaller and smaller.

Back in the cold air, Mert tightened her scarf. She said, "*That* was interesting. What did you think?"

"I don't know," I said miserably, "what did you?"

Mert said, "Well, *first* of all, I'm not sure I buy the body-language theory. I think it's misleading. Because, for instance, some of those women couldn't cross their legs if they tried. They're too—large. Does that make them more receptive to other people's feelings and ideas? Or does it simply mean they're too fat to cross their legs?" She loosened and reknotted the scarf, and sighed. "But if that group is useful for you—if it's helping—"

"Not really," I said.

Mert nodded. "You're much smarter than that counselor, anyway. What's she going to tell you that you don't already know?"

THERE MUST ALWAYS be someone to watch the body, ensure it won't do the wrong thing: bulge too far, shrink too near. If I could have picked a body to be in, it would have been a man's. That straight-down-ness, that bony plunge. In a chap-husk my thighs wouldn't chafe; they would be lean and long and ready to run me away from machete or mastodon.

AT THE HISTORY museum we leaned on the cold wall, and the lemon smell of the floor became a taste. Cam kissed fast, fingers tight on my neck. He pressed me to the marble. Instead of kissing back, I had to talk: "How come all these tourists who never go to museums in their regular lives go to a million when they're on vacation?"

"Who the fuck cares," he whispered.

"I don't know, *me*?"—tugging his hand out from under my jacket.

"You are bound," Mr. Nzambi told him, "for great things." He asked where he planned to apply next year. "Good," he nodded when Cam said the big names. Our high school, a crappy public factory, was a disadvantage. "But your recommendations will be outstanding," Mr. Nzambi consoled. "And if your SAT scores are anything like your PSATs…"

Our teacher smiled, and I watched the hot reed grow taller in Cam's throat. I could tell he was seeing himself pink-nosed in snowy northern twilight, books on his back, crossing what was known as a green.

My parents liked Cam, despite his alarming (in their opinion) outfits, because he was polite and good at school. In the six months we went so-called *out*, I tried to limit their contact with him, but contact happened. He got invited to dinner, where he asked Fod—grown-up style—about his research. He mentioned a novel he was reading, and Mert dove gratefully in; the two chattered like teeth in love, while I, who had never read the book in question, toe-pinched my brother under the table.

Their approval made me like Cam less.

Which made me a cliché, I guess.

I ANSWERED THE phone in the juvenile manner I only dared use when Riley was at work: "Den of Coyote, how may we help you?"

A man's voice said, "Quinn?"

"Yeah?"

"It's Cameron."

"Shit," I said. "I mean, hi!"

"Hello," he said. He sounded neither pleased nor displeased, friendly nor unfriendly.

"You got my letter."

"I did."

"Great," I said, snapping the rubber band hard.

"Do you want to meet for a coffee?" said this man whose name was Cameron.

"Sure," I shouted, so nervous I had no volume control.

"Okay," he said.

"When? My schedule's very open."

"This week's not good, but how about next Wednesday?"

The voice betrayed nothing: he could have been a salesman, a business acquaintance, a doctor's office.

Then I smoked three cigarettes in a row, and still felt like I was shouting, but no sound was coming out.

"**IF STRANDED IN** the Himalayas and your foot got frost-bite, which you'd know by"—the middle squinted at the notebook—"*skin that is pale and waxy and the bitten part feels like a piece of wood,* what would you do?"

"Chop it off and save the rest of me," said the oldest.

"Make a fire and hold the foot over the fire until it melted enough to walk on," said the youngest.

"The pain of melting would be exquisite," said the middle.

"I wouldn't mind a fake foot," said the oldest. "I'd look like a sea captain."

The middle said, "But your teeth are too clean to look like one."

IT WAS FOD, not Mert, waiting outside the good doctor's building.

"Don't you have class?"

He smiled. "I cancelled it."

"What for?" I latched my seat belt.

"Because I wanted to pick you up."

"Why?"

"Just to hang out."

I laughed. "Hang *out*?"

"Sure, why not? We don't get to see each other all that much."

I said nothing, not sure this was true. He was usually at dinner, wasn't he?

"So," he said, "how was your session?"

"Fine."

"She's helpful, the doctor?"

"Yeah she's good."

"What sorts of things do you talk about?" He was acting so weird it made me want to get out of the car.

"Things," I said.

He rushed: "You don't have to be thin for us to love you!"

"I know, Fod," I whispered, shoving my face to the window.

"We love you exactly the way you are. I mean, however much you weigh."

"I *know*."

Had my mother given him instructions? How could I tell them—make them know the real—*correct* them—

"You're a fantastic kid," Fod added.

How was I supposed to make them believe that I was not trying to be thinner, only trying to stop bleeding? I couldn't, and so would endure their Afterschool Specialness.

THE FIRST THING Pine said was, "Does either of you hate asparagus?"

"Is that what we're having?" asked Riley.

"Only if you like it."

"It's my preferred vegetable," I said, already wishing this plan had never come to fruition.

"Come into my parlor," said Pine.

"Nice apron," I told her.

"You like it?" She smoothed it over her knees. "It was my dear grandmother's. Well, not really—the one grandmother couldn't cook to save her pitted northern soul, and the other was so effing tight she didn't leave a red *centime*, much less an apron, to any of her issue. Would you like a beverage?"

Twelve bites only. *Stop counting.* No more than twelve. *Stop counting.*

Pine said nothing about the asparagus left on my plate. It got swept briskly into the garbage. She presented us with a tangerine cake so shapely it was hard to believe she had baked it herself. (She might have been lying.) My brother, helping himself to a third piece, got crumbs all over the joint. Pine stalled his napkin hand with a pale finger.

"Don't wipe like that, they'll smear; wipe like *this*."

Riley laughed. "You're as bossy as our sister."

"Was she a domineerer?"

"Yeah, always organizing everything."

Pine chomped a tangerine forkful. I sensed her beady eyes on my undrunk tea. "Too strong?" she inquired.

"No, it's fine. Very, um, British-tasting."

"Sometimes I make it darker than people on this side of the Atlantic have a taste for."

"Don't worry about it," I said.

Riley, on whom small human tensions were less lost than they were on the average male, swooped in with diversion. "So when are you finally going to tell us your real name?"

She shrugged, said matter-of-factly: "Pine is my middle name. My first name is Crannog."

"Um, wow."

"It means lake dweller," she explained. "I was christened after a remote ancestor famous for his ill-starred courage. Hundreds of years ago in the Highlands, he declined to send forward the fire cross."

"The *quoi*?"

"A fire cross is a symbol in Scotland for calling the nation to arms. The tips get burnt black, and bits of it are smeared with blood, and it's carried from one village, castle, or sheep hill to another to rouse the men. If you refuse to keep it going or to rise to arms, the last person to have it shoots you dead. Well, my cousin refused. He did not think the cause was just."

"What was the cause?"

"Nobody remembers," Pine said. "All we know is he believed it was in error—and threw the fire cross down on the peat. Took a bullet in the brain."

You fucking bitch, said the back of my mouth. But how was she supposed to know? Riley probably hadn't told her the details.

"So he's a brave person to be named after," Riley concluded.

"Wasted on me, I'm afraid. I have a crippling fear of wood ticks and my idea of adventure is watching people make béarnaise sauce on television." Pine smiled and tapped my brother's knuckles. "Why is your hand always going over your mouth? Like a messenger afraid of getting killed."

"I didn't know I do that," Riley said. *He thought he stopped doing that.* He brushed his lips with the tips of three fingers. "Is this how?"

"No," she said, "more like this…" and adjusted his palm flat across his mouth.

They were practically having sex right in front of me. Riley needed to get on that, pronto. She was clearly willing. Why hadn't he made any move? The gene pool that had given our sister her *If he tries to punch me he'll get it in the eye with scissors* had been drained of guts by the time Riley's egg began to grow.

Back at headquarters, I remarked on the tastiness of the dinner and forced myself to add: "Pine seems like a nice person."

Riley blushed, setting down a pile of sheets, blanket, and pillow. "Tell me if you need more blanket."

"I'll be fine. Thanks again, Coyote—I swear, it'll be very temporary—this is extremely great of you—"

He was at the sink filling the kettle, but even from behind I could tell what he was thinking: *Fake-sweet! Fake-good-mannered!* He called, "You want tea?"

But we'd just had tea. "Anything stronger, perchance?"

"No," he said.

"Then sure." I would do like the Romans.

Stain-free pillows, can of flowers, heavy shining wood table, swept floor: my brother had an agreeable nest, so much more comfortable than my abodes had ever been. I was jealous, but proud too. He could shoot a good photograph; he could make a good room.

And tea. It smelled pretty.

"Don't put it there!" he yelped. "It'll leave a—"

I grabbed at the cup.

"No, wait—it's fine—I'm sorry—you can put it down. It's okay."

My hand hovered in midair.

"Sorry, yeah, don't worry about it!"

I frowned, set the tea back on the table.

"Sorry," he repeated.

THE NEW YEAR'S party was a huge one thrown by a famous local outfit at their compound near the zoo. Pete knew about it from his older girlfriend, who got wind of all the good parties even though she didn't play in a band or do, really, much at all except carve griffins out of dump-salvaged wood. Cam and I trailed behind Pete into the hot throng, proud to be among so many luminaries at the home of such a notorious band. It sent a shiver up the back of my throat to brush in a hallway the same shoulder that had been wearing a guitar when I'd seen them play—or to meet, across a kitchen, the same eyes that had glared down from the park stage last summer. Cam and I had been talking about starting a band ourselves, and maybe we actually would; and maybe people would know of us one day. Kids at a party would thrill to recognize me. Once you were notorious, all you had to do was stand there in your skin.

Ten minutes before midnight, Cam couldn't find me. We never touched in public, only in my parents' basement, but tonight was New Year's: he wanted to kiss. None of the teeming little rooms contained me. Five minutes left. Upstairs to check again. One minute left. Downstairs, they were roaring the countdown: Twenty-six . . . twenty-five . . . Then he saw a ladder he hadn't noticed earlier. The third floor was black and raw, an attic. The two bodies in the corner were gasping loud enough not to hear his feet on the rungs. A lurchy cheer from below: the fresh year. He said my name forlornly, and waited to see who the boy was.

ON WEDNESDAY I waited the whole day inside. I smoked many cigarettes. I washed dishes and cut my toenails and played several rounds of Wake Up the Sister. The appointment was a black splotch at 6:00 PM; we were to meet near the university. "It's a new place," he'd said on the phone. "Kind of funky."

The walls and floor were orange, the ceiling green. Like being inside a pumpkin. Early, I chose a seat in the corner so that no one was behind me. At the condiment counter two dirt-children, boy and girl, were making oatmeal. They had brought their own packets, which they stirred into cups of hot water (tea was the cheapest menu item) and improved with free sugar and cinnamon. Against the wall were piled backpacks, sleeping bags, soil-stiff glimmies. They were speechlessly intent on the oatmeal—long enough with each other, I guessed, that conversation wasn't necessary. The kids made me wistful, but it wasn't Cam I missed: it was the untethered life. Every day you woke up and could go somewhere you'd never been. Strike out for the territory. The road was fast under you. If you didn't like a place, you left.

The oatmeals were now discussing a show they'd seen last week, how incredible the sound was, how it was weird they had played so much stuff from the first record and that they'd worn red life-size wings. Their voices had a fluty calm, broken now and then by laughter; they were relaxed in the knowledge that they'd see another incredible show soon, and if not soon, eventually.

I knew, had known, so many names. They used to stand on shelves in my brain, easily reached for. One had led to another: Yeah but have you heard the band he was in *before*, they were called— Have you heard. Have you seen. Do you know. Then, a name: and the name had said a lot about you, if the other person knew enough to decode it. What good did it do me now to know the name of the third drummer for . . . , to have seen the second-ever show of . . . , or to own an original pressing of the first album of . . . ? Our manager, Uncle Seven, had never failed to be impressed by all I knew, because it was a male expertise. In his own day, girls had filled out the audience.

Two people could be a tribe unto themselves. These dirt-children were. They roamed as a unit, unafraid because together. The boy picked an oatmeal flake off the girl's chin. She handed him a lighter as he headed out to smoke. Secure in the certainty he would return, she turned her attention to a small pink notebook. She was trying to quit, herself, so she wrote instead. She chronicled their adventures. *Here we are in not the world's coolest city but I like it sort of.*

I saw Cam come through the door. He looked fuller. Not fat, just—filled. His cheeks no longer slanted inward. Encasing his now-solid legs was the kind of father-pant denim he'd once have committed suicide before wearing in public. But his hair was the same: black and shiny, old-fashioned, excellent.

A hearty smile parted my lips and I got to my feet. "Hi!"

"Hi," he said, slowing down. We were not going to hug. He arranged himself in the green seat across from me. "Hope this is all right? We have to go up to the counter—no table service."

His hands had gone straight into his lap.

I wanted badly to smoke.

"So you look good," he said.

I wondered if he was making fun of me. Of course I did not look good. Econo-chic, which everyone back in the day had hurried to master, was now for me actually true—and it didn't age so nicely. Too old to be chic, I was gruesomely econo. I ate frozen burritos and not enough vegetables. I wore old britches, old button-downs, corduroy jackets that did not become me. Cam, on the other hand, looked like a grown-up who went to the gym, flossed daily, and ate plenty of greens. His running times and mortgage rates were down; his bowling scores and IRAs were up.

"How's your little brother?" he said.

"Crazy as ever. And still a virgin, I think."

He smiled, much like someone's parent at a piano recital. I reached to snap, but my wrist was bare. He said, "You coming from work?"

"Um, no, I'm not. You?"

"Yeah, I taught a seminar this afternoon, then met with a couple of students." He was keeping his hands in his lap.

I stormed my brain for something to say.

He smiled, too stretchily. "You want to get some food, or—?"

"Sure, totally. I can go order for us—what do you—I mean, coffee, or—?"

"No, no," he said, "I'll go—"

"No, seriously, it's fine—"

Together we marched to the counter, staring straight ahead.

I HEARD CAM say my name. He was a black shape by the stairs. Pete and I hadn't undressed so it didn't take long to cover ourselves. "Hey," I squeaked. My brains were beating hard. Pete started to lift his face but I shoved it down, wanting to delay as long as possible the moment when Cam understood the size of the betrayal.

He didn't speak to me again until the start of senior year. I had long since stopped fooling around with Pete, whose devotion to the griffin carver proved irritatingly strong.

I found a note in my locker: *Even though you kicked me in the fucking heart I have decided we can be friends again.*

Our first activity of being friends again was a trip to the convenience store. I bought a frostee for him, licorice for myself. "Those socks are so awesome," I said. "They match your suspenders!"

"Shut up, Quinn," Cam said.

Our second activity was me learning that he was going out with Clarissa Smith, a girl I hated. He delivered the news so casually you'd never have known—although I did know—how much he was relishing it.

"I've never felt this way about anyone before," he said, and it worked. That is, it hurt.

ONCE THE COFFEES were steaming in front of us, our bodies again in their careful cross-table hunches, I wanted to scream or laugh. Maybe howl. Cackle? What would Cam do if I began cackling and refused to stop?

"So are…"

"Sorry?"

"Are you still playing music?" he said loudly.

"Oh no. No no no no. It hurts my ears." Without thinking, I added, "How about you?"

He held up his left hand. It was pale and smooth and empty; he could have been making a fist. The fingers could have been hiding. The thumbnail, I saw, was clean. "Makes it a little difficult," he said.

"I'm sorry," I said.

"For what?"

I scrunched my cheeks.

He waited.

"For that incredibly stupid question."

Cam nodded. We cleared our throats and sipped our coffees. For the next fifty-two minutes our talk was entirely small. I spoke of the bookstore and its demise; he described being a tax attorney and how it differed, in ways good and bad, from teaching tax law. Our parents were asked after and reported to be fine. Romantic statuses were touched upon: me, a dry season; him, a girlfriend of three years he hadn't gotten around to proposing to. She was a lawyer too, but not tax.

At the fifty-third minute, he apologized for a dinner meeting he needed to get to, adding that it was great to see me and he hoped I would take care.

"WHAT WOULD WE be called, though?" Cam said.

"I've been making a list," I said.

"It can't be mediocre or grows-on-you. Has to be instantly recognizable as good."

"My list is long," I said.

"And who's going to play guitar?"

"Me, of course."

"Are you serious?"

"Fuck off," I said. "And Clarissa is not going to play tambourine, or anything else for that matter."

"Never said she was." Cam smiled. "Her talents lie elsewhere."

THE NIGHT HAS *eyes in northern wilds: black bowl of stars, peeks of animals on parking lot fringe. I write in the dark while others lose greel inside. On some native reservation in midst of nothing. Day off and everyone in bad moods and it's either get drunk which is not new or gamble which is more novelty. Gecko was the most excited all huffy blowing dog breath right in my face. He goes I'm'a throw us a windfall since we're not making anything any other way! But he doesn't know since we haven't told him about the Offer. Only C and me know. I think about it a lot but don't talk since that's crass and annoys C who is worried, very worried about my sellout potential.*

I'D EXPECTED TO give the Cam coffee report to Mink or Geck, but I found myself wanting to tell Riley.

The morning bird was rust quivering on a lash. Hello, bird. What kind are you? I knew no names, only the colors they made. A cat screaming at night was a fling of red. Cat and bird lived together in the red department. Riley's name belonged to the blue department; my own belonged to the black. Rinsed sky, finger branches, window glass hot on my cheek. People on the street were happy it was the weekend and not raining anymore. They had flocked here to shop and to stroll. They were flirting. They were going for brunch. The radio puffed out its tame Sunday smoke—harpsichord, clavier.

I missed my old neighborhood, which never had shoppers. I wondered how Two Thumbs was doing. Had his nub wound healed? Did he mourn the loss of its powers?

Pine had been a twig on Riley's couch all morning, reading a book about dirigibles while she waited for cups of poison to kill the roaches in her kitchen. "Did you know," she called, "that during World War I the German military and its abettor, Count Zeppelin, thought they'd found in the dirigible the perfect weapon to sink the British navy?"

"I did *not* know," said Riley, sweeping a floor that was already quite clean.

"Well, the fact was, zeppelins were almost totally ineffectual as bomb throwers. They were stymied by cloud and darkness. The damage they inflicted in the war was negligible."

"Do you want to have brunch?" he said.

"You don't have much food," she pointed out.

"No I mean we could go somewhere." Riley turned back to the street. "Look, Quinn, see that dungeony person? He goes to Mrs. Jones constantly. He is like her best customer."

I glanced down.

"Hey wait a minute," I said.

"Do you see him? He loves fortunes."

"Yeah and I *saw* him—like, just the other day—on Observatory."

"How can you tell it was the same person?"

"Well, how many people wear hooded capes who aren't in movies about racism?"

Maybe I'd been a little neezled at my parents', furnished myself a false memory? Déjà vu in reverse.

If you were introduced to the dungeoner, what would you say? If you asked the dungeoner why he wears a hood, how would the dungeoner reply? If the dungeoner is not a he but a she, how would—

"All right, I'm done with this chapter," Pine said, stretching. "Let's brunch ourselves into a coma." Jesus, would she never leave us? "Do you want to come, Quinn?"

"You two go," I said, hoping Riley would notice my wanting-to-talk face and opt to stay.

"Okay," he said. "See you."

"RILEY, GET YOUR hand away from your mouth; it's really not very becoming."

"I said—"

"*What?* I cannot understand you when you speak through your fingers."

"If she was alive, she would be old enough to get her driver's license."

"*Were* alive," Mert corrected.

She ladled stew onto Fod's plate, then my brother's and mine and her own.

I went on peeling my thumb.

Riley said, louder, "She would've turned sixteen this year."

Fod said, "This tastes wonderful!"

"Cilantro," Mert explained, "and garlic, plenty of garlic."

"Wonderful," Fod repeated.

I laid three peels next to my plate and waited for them to notice.

She, she, she. Never the name.

"HEY I GOT in!" Cam yelled through the phone.

I said nothing.

"Hello?"

"I'm here."

"Well aren't you glad for me? I fucking *got in*."

"Sure," I said, "but how can we start our band if you're all the way up in New England?"

Another silence, longer. Then he said, "Oh."

"I mean, I know it's an incredible school and all. So, whatever."

"Maybe I could defer a year," he said.

"SORRY," MINK SAID, "but no."

"You have to! It's the *law.*"

"Geck, you're already drunk. I'm not—"

"Your job is to serve beverage to people who can pay for it, and I can pay for it, and I am not drunk. Breathalyze me!"

She walked to the other end of the bar, wiping her lip on her sleeve, humming one note.

"Please, Mink?"

He had been doing good for a while. He had been looking better.

"Mink!" he hollered. "Fucking come give me a drink!"

Her face was in her hand.

"Hey Geckers," I called down the bar.

He was painstakingly counting a tiny sheaf of cash. "Hold on, I'm getting a—"

"I don't think you are," I said. "Let's take a turn around the neighborhood."

"Turn?"

"A walk. Come take a walk with me."

"What for?"

"Our healths."

I prodded him off the stool; he didn't put up much of a fight, though he grumbled: "It'll be all cold."

"It's seventy degrees out."

"God*dammit*," he said.

I slowed my stride to match the shamble of his bad leg. It was a weeknight, so not crowded, and late enough that most storefronts were dark. "Might be good to hit a meeting tomorrow," I told him. "You still going to those?"

"*Those*," he muttered.

"They were helping for a while, right?"

"Yeah, they helped me *throw up* because of so much complaining. I swear to the Lord, you want some cheese with that whine? It's all just bitches bitching and that midget eating cashews from a ziplock. And some sparklers who think it's *awesome* to be addicts but aren't really. And, like, a guy talking for nine hours about how he ate so many hot wings one summer he started bleeding from his butt and had to wear an anal tampon. Is that really worth discussing?"

"Well, maybe it is to him."

Geck snorted and pulled up short, fishing in his jacket for a deck.

It was safe to assume he would not find one. I handed him a cigarette.

"Ta, as the British say. Anyhoo, where the fuck are we going? I don't even know where I'm laying my head tonight. The familial compound is far far far. At some hour the buses stop running."

"You can sleep at my brother's. But only this one time."

"Tight," he said.

I woke to him in a heap on the floor, body pretzeled and yellow hair ahoo. He had slept the very same way on Nebraska couch, Minnesota pool table, Ohio café linoleum, Wisconsin turret rug. When I stuck out a leg to kick him, I was alarmed to see how thick my calf hairs had grown.

He grunted, "Whut."

"Time to exit before you are seen."

But Riley padded in, smiling, then not smiling when he noticed the blanketful of body.

"Hello?"

"Don't be afraid," I said, "it's only Geck."

"Hi Riley!" he yelled from underneath.

"On your way to the salt mines?" I asked.

My brother nodded. "About tonight—want to meet at F-D-E?"

"What for?"

"Observatory Place."

"Shit. I forgot."

"See you then, then?"

"Yes, captain."

Geck climbed out from under the blanket. "What the fuck is F-D-E?"

"Six forty-five," I explained. "It's a code for time."

"Nerfy." He stretched, yawned. "What about some coffee?"

"What about it."

"Like why don't you make some?"

"Not a restaurant," I said.

"One cup of jehosophat for an old comrade? You have an urgent appointment or some shit?"

"I have things to do."

He laughed. "What, like not work?"

"I'm waiting on some leads."

"Right. Me too." He stood up, and I saw his member hanging out of the boxers, in all its uncircumcised glory.

"Jesus, Geck."

"What?"

"Put that *away*."

"Oh!" He swiveled, rearranging himself, and stomped to the bathroom.

I filled the kettle. He was big, I'd give him that. Bigger than anyone I'd ever slept with, except for that kneesocked kid in Arkansas. I couldn't help comparing, once upon a time, Geck's pizzle to Cam's. One uncut, bulky, brown; the other pink and willowy. In Milwaukee, right before the accident, I had held Cam's and thought about Geck's.

Geck slurped his coffee like a wood-hog.

"So I saw Cam," I said.

"Did you say hello?"

"No, we hung *out*. In a planned way."

Into his cup he dumped another spoonload of sugar. "No shit. Wow." He did not sound sufficiently impressed.

"It'd been ten *years*," I reminded him.

"Was he balding?"

"What?"

"I bet he's lost some of that goddamn hair, right?"

"Actually, his hair is still great."

"Oh."

"And he didn't seem mad at me," I added. "We just talked about current events."

Geck shrugged. "You can't always tell with that guy. As I recall, he had a tendency to be emotionally stealth."

CAM FROWNED WHEN the yellow-haired boy came up the alley carrying a hardcase—we were outside taking a break—and said hello in a voice that was higher than you'd expect. I had invited him without telling. "Come on in!" I cried, and Cam was speechless, and Mink fluffed back her hair. Geck took out his guitar, a lime-and-white hollow body with a scarred black pickguard, and he said, "Want to play one of your songs and I'll figure something out?"

"He's fucking fantastic!" I said later.

"I wouldn't go *that* far," Cam said, shoving his hand into the potato chip can.

At first I reassured myself that it was the combination, the combustible parts together, that made a band; you could not isolate one part and say *That* is what we owe it to!—rather, everyone was necessary. But the honest part of me knew, ever since the first song Geck wrote, that he was the reason we started getting somewhere. Something about his guitar.

We faced them together, slicing their breath, hands fast, we swayed together hip-high in the noise, the audience dragged us out, reaching, reaching, we stayed down and away from the regular day. But we *are* secretly normal, Cam said, we are these normal people who rinse dishes and take shits and want houses. I don't want a house, I said. Our van was the freight car, our backpacks the kerchiefed stick. On stages we did not need to look at each other. And Geck made us buyable, and Mink made us photogenic. Her prettiness wasn't her fault, but it was the only thing she added. Anyone can play three notes for three minutes. She stood like a statue, drawing the eyes. Every band needs a beautiful girl, Uncle Seven said. He did not say beautiful *girls*.

NORMALLY WE'D GOTTEN spanked on the bottom or slapped in the face, but once, when Riley was in third grade, Fod had punched him straight in the stomach. My brother had been so stunned he didn't cry, at first. He couldn't breathe enough to make a sound. We watched his throat stretch for air.

"Poor Coyote," my sister said, resting a hand on his belly button. "Does it hurt still?"

Riley nodded.

"He's so terrible," she said with relish. "I can't wait till Mert comes home."

"But you can't tell!"

"Why not?"

Riley shrugged, shutting his eyes. "I don't want you to."

"But Ri, he's *terrible.*"

Riley coughed.

"See, he punctured your lung. I hate him," she declared. "If he ever tries to punch *me* I'll do him a mischief. He'll get it in the eye—with scissors."

And I thought, As soon as I'm tall enough…

But the Edinburgh Lane doorway of pencil marks ended up no use. I never grew as tall as my father. By the time I had concluded I was stuck where I was, not yet unassailable, Fod had stopped assailing. No measurements were ever taken on Observatory Place. It was a smaller house, one of many brick boxes; but there was still a garden for the non-football months, and the TV was huge. My parents were not television people, they were book people—so they always said—though I suspected Mert of watching parlor mysteries when Fod wasn't around, and Fod, maybe, of ordering a bit of pay-per-view when—

"Dinner in five minutes," Mert called to me.

Mother in the kitchen, rattling. Father in the garden, plucking. Son at the table, setting. Daughter in the living room, flipping. It was still light out and birds talked near the window. I landed on history, a nice channel because most of the topics were remote. "Dragon's teeth," the announcer announced, "was the name for pyramids of fortified concrete used in World War II to herd tanks into killing zones where they could be picked off by antitank weaponry. Each tooth was four feet high, and land mines were often planted between them. Because so many were built and they were so durable, rows of dragon's teeth can be seen today in Germany and France."

"Quinn, time to eat!"

"Hold on," I shouted.

"In Switzerland," added the announcer, "they are still used as strategic defensive devices—designed to spring up, for instance, out of roads—and are called *toblerone* after the chocolate bar."

"Turn it off, please."

How much is a one-way ticket from the airport to the Fourteenth Street bridge?

Turn that crap off!

But Mert, it's funny—

Making fun of people dying is funny?

I slid into the chair and poured myself a glass of white. Waited as long as possible to take food; the worm was near.

"So, Coyote," started Mert in the fake-casual voice, "anytime you'd like to invite your, ah, friend from work to have dinner with us, you're welcome to. I heard that she made a very nice meal for you and Quinn."

My brother's eyes swerved to me, furious.

"Hey Mert, what's in this soup? It's an intriguing blend of flavors. Did you use dill? It tastes sort of *dillish*."

"I did indeed," she said.

"Dill was her most hated herb," I remarked.

"Pass the okra," said Fod.

"She really couldn't stand it, remember? Said it was like having porcupine eyelashes in your food."

Our father thanked our mother for passing the okra.

"How has work been going?" Mert asked Riley.

But I would push an inch more: "My point is, she would *not* have been a fan of this soup."

HELLO, IS THIS Air Florida? Can you tell me the fare for a one-way ticket from the airport to the Fourteenth Street bridge?

But the joke wasn't funny, because a man had given a woman the rope instead of taking it himself. He waited for her to be pulled up into the helicopter. Another woman next—he helped her hands catch the swinging cable—and he waited too long, went blue in the ice-chunked water. Frozen pressure sensors had caused the aircraft to stop short in the sky. Nobody had turned on the plane's anti-icing systems, even though it was a frosty January day. Dead: seventy passengers, four crew, four motorists on the bridge. Alive: one crew member and four passengers, including the women the dead man guided to the rope.

"WHAT WERE YOU doing?"

"Nothing."

"Yes you were—your face is all—" I took her fist and pried it open. Sandpaper, red-smeared. "You were sanding your *face*?"

My sister shrugged.

"What for?"

She touched her bleeding cheek. "To get the pimples off."

RILEY IN YELLOW-DUCK boxers loomed up in the doorway. "You can't smoke in here!"

"Oh, what?" I mashed out the butt in my teacup.

"*God,*" he said, waving a hand in front of his face, spinsterlike.

"Sorry, I forgot."

"No you didn't. You didn't *care.*"

"That's not—"

"Open a window," he said, and slammed back into the bedroom.

Octy watched me pop in the cartridge, finish off one can and crack another while it loaded. Much skill, I informed him, was required for this particular contest. Perfect eyesight, hair-trigger reflexes, and *courage.* Bravery was key. The night was cold. The snow was coming. Ice everywhere, but you couldn't see it. Did you know that about ice, Octy? The octopus stared back. Well, you might not have to deal with this in the ocean, but on land, ice impersonates the road. You're tooling along thinking it's a road but really it's a rink. See, look—

The game began: two black lanes, headlights, your fingers pale on the wheel. The road twisted through a forest. Above, stars, but it wasn't advisable to look up. Keep your eyes on the. Keep your speed under the. Don't reach down to change the. Don't be drunk when you.

NEW TO THE band, Geck had never gone with us to the diner and didn't know the rule. We didn't hear him order because I was too busy slapping water on the small fire I had made from ashing into a napkin and it wasn't his fault, as Mink reasoned later, because how could he possibly have known?

I lifted my head, alert like a hunting animal; the waitress hadn't even reached our table but I could smell what she was carrying, the death on her arm, sizzle of cooked sister.

"What the *fuck*, did somebody get pancakes?"

"I did," Geck said uncuriously.

"You what?"

"Blueberry," he nodded.

The waitress was about to set down the plate but I pushed it away and it sailed to the carpet.

"Christ," said the waitress.

"That was my *food*," said Geck.

"I'm still charging you for that," she warned.

"Fucking fine," I said, flicking and flicking the rubber band.

The first song Geck wrote for us went into heavy rotation on college stations. They screamed for it at shows. Our *hit*. Cam hated the song because it was the kind of thing we had promised each other, at the start, never to play: catch and froth, as close to sugar as we would ever get. We did not play it sweetly; I grunted, shouted, refused to actually sing; yet it could not be anything but a sing-along song. It made people who had never heard it feel as if they'd heard it before—to hum with it, mouth lyrics when they didn't know them, and to declare at once *Oh I love this one, what it's called again?* I knew it was second-rate but could not hate it, because it sent us into every basement in America, and the record sold so well that the scouts began to sniff.

I IMAGINED HIM on his plaid-spread single bed under a shelf of elementary-school swimming trophies, toes brushing a carpet dusty with shed skin. He sipped from a plastic cup of vodka and strummed his guitar. His fingers were clumsy, getting fatter like the rest of him. Thank you, tapioca! Thank you, plum-sauced brisket! Dejected, Geck got the cane from under his bed. Rubbed its brass knob. He had not believed at first that the cane had really been made from a bull's diddler, but the gift giver had sworn it was genuine beef-cock. They used taxidermy, he explained, to cure the tissue, then they stretched it over a metal rod. Geck had been impressed; the cane was three and a half feet long. What happened to the balls? They made them into Rocky Mountain oysters, his buddy said.

"Jonathan? Dear? Quinn is on the phone."

He knotted the drawstring on his sweatpants. "Medicine woman!" he jovialed into the receiver.

"Never call me that," I said.

"Sorry, sorry. How are you?"

"Fine, you?"

"Not good. Thanks for never calling me back."

"We're on the phone right now," I pointed out.

"Yeah, after *three days*." I could hear him taking an-other sip. "So, want to go to a meeting with me?"

My neck flinched: what was he implying?

"I keep slipping," he went on, "and the likelihood of me getting to a meeting improves rapidly if another per-son goes with me."

"Such as your sponsor," I said, relieved.

"Such as *you*. Come on, Quinn, I don't have that many friends."

The commute to his neck of the woods—train and bus and walk through grummy dusk—took over an hour. Geck's parents were retired enough to live in Florida but didn't. The living room smelled of old people's mouths. Mrs. Geck asked if I wanted something to drink; Geck shooed her away before I could answer.

"May I offer you a nail," he said, "for the lovely box your coffin is sure to be?"

I stuck it between my teeth, slapped my jacket for matches. He was already on my nerves. That tends to happen if you've slept with a person, no matter how long ago: your irritation threshold is lower.

"Jonathan," came a call from the next room, "would you like some cookies?"

"No, Ma," he shouted, "we're fine."

"I wouldn't mind a cookie," I said.

"Yeah, well, you don't get one. She *hovers* like a god-damn chopper."

Out on the sidewalk, I asked, "Isn't it against the rules to be drunk at a meeting?"

"Are you drunk?"

"I'm serious, Geck, can't they kick you out?"

"*Hail* no. The only requirement for membership is a desire to stop drinking. As long as you don't cause disturbance, you can be as fucked up as you want. Which, by the way, I am not. Just because I'm not acting suicidal doesn't mean I'm—"

"But you've obviously had a few."

"A few does not drunkenness make."

"Pick up the pace. We'll be late."

"Good," he said. "It's fucking misery-town up in there."

The church basement smelled like burnt chicken. A circle of souls on folding chairs. Everyone stared at this one woman, who was sniffling: "One spoonful! I told myself one spoonful…"

"She likes to party with the cough syrup," Geck leaned to whisper. His breath was shocking.

"Is your sponsor here?"

"Um…" He craned around, subtle as a hammer. His eyes stopped on a woman with some of the profoundest cleavage I'd ever seen in person.

I elbowed his elbow.

"I don't see him," he hissed.

The syrup eater thanked us for listening, and now it was a baseball-capped kid, who said: "I've been getting suggestions from people to just go ahead and spill it, stop keeping secrets and just hand it over to the group and to my higher power. I know the definition of insanity is doing the same thing over and over and expecting different results, so I'm, like I said, trying something new and opening up a little, even though I'm really…"

"Arrive at the point!" spat Geck, fingering his pockets. Suddenly he stood, and I was afraid he would outright leave, which seemed bad, especially as the boy had just begun sharing about sexual molestation; but he was only headed to the refreshment table. He returned with a fistful of beige cookies, dropped two into my lap, and whispered, "Pecan sandies. Lowest of the low."

"YOU WILL REGRET this," Cam said. "It won't end well."

I forked a bite of coleslaw. "What the hell do *you* know."

"Well, I know that you sleeping with our guitar player is a bad idea."

It was six months after Geck had joined.

"We're not doing it in *front* of you."

"It tends to cause problems," he said.

"No problems so far," I shrugged.

"Except maybe for you. The embarrassment of having sex with someone who has a fifth-grade vocabulary?"

"*What?*"

"I mean, doesn't it get a little lonely?"

"Fuck you," I said.

He stood, pocketed his deck, and walked out of the diner without leaving a cent.

"Little baby," I called after him.

A scout from the label was blithering on about how much she liked us, and Cam said, "My lady kind of doth protest too much!" and she paused, first confused, then irritated. After we left the bar I whispered: "If you wreck this, I'm never speaking to you again."

I was quite advanced in the maturity department.

And for three days we didn't talk. He was stunned that I would put so much faith in a raggly little scout who, after all, was not making any signing decisions; she could only recommend; but I believed that this label, a major less evil than the others whose stable included bands we respected, was heaven-sent. More than dollars: it meant we would be known by everyone—kids on farms!—not just outcasts and aficionados.

Cam told me I was venal, and I had to later look up *venal* in the dictionary that sat under a speaker in the Belfry Street living room.

I RESORTED TO knife. *Blood came. I couldn't stand the nnnnhhhhhh NNNNNNHHHHH! and I took my little blade and shoved it in. Afterward looked like stunt pulled by some sicki-fied spark imitating that painter, but it wasn't, since I didn't expect the blood I only wanted to cut out the ringing. It is still there as I write this, going*

nnnnnnnnnnnnnhhhhhhhhhhhhh

NNNNNNNNNNNHHHHHHHHHH!

I saw this article about other musicians who have it (there's in fact a lot) with little quotes by their names about how they've just gotten used to it or how it used to drive them cra-zy but now they're so rich they don't notice. When blood ran down my neck Cam noticed. Shit what'd you do??? He got a napkin and cleaned my neck and my ear's hot shell.

ME AND A man and a curtain. He hid behind the tall red pleats until I'd finished taking my sweatpants off. Red streaks marbled the milk of his shoulders. He swelled toward me. It was plain he would kill me, but not before we fucked. I did not try to get away. I loved the thick full feel of him driving up my downstairs, hitting the mouth of my cervix, again and again.

I was making materials the uterus discards. The discarded body went on a shelf, then into a box. The box was lowered. After the worm ate the body, there was no more to eat. Worm licked bone to white. A worm was a tongue. Each month, an egg came down. Did a chicken have a uterus?

A worm was a foot and a stomach. The bloodworm's eyes were grown over with skin. It nibbled sightlessly, taking its time. First the tender lining of the mouth. Lacustrina had had the head of a girl and the legs of a snake.

Does the worm live in your vagina? The good doctor could be so stupid. Worms did not live in vaginas. Bugs did—if you slept with certain guys, later you might find bugs in the hair—but the bloodworm didn't. It had been too hard to explain. I'd hated that look the good doctor got when she didn't get it.

WE SAT IN the kitchen, rainy morning, toast and jam. I took my chance. "So, Ri, how's your love life?"

One eye slitted and his freckles heated from brown to red. He put his fingers over his mouth.

"Um," he finally said.

I nodded encouragingly.

"I don't know," he said. "Will you give me the butter?"

"The Pinecone, right? You like her?"

He shrugged.

"You do, right?"

"Kind of, but I don't know if *she* does and we're friends so I don't want to mess it up and it would be the worst if I tried to kiss her and she didn't want to kiss me back."

His face was so red that I would have laughed if I hadn't been weirdly on the verge of tears.

I cleared my throat and said, "It would also be the worst if you didn't try, right? Maybe you guys would be really happy if you got together. Maybe not, of course— but the maybe yes is the important one."

He nervously smiled, the green of his eyes like a shoot on the forest floor.

MY BROTHER WENT with us to the diner the day we left for the *Purgastoria* tour. It was a Wednesday but we ordered massive Sunday breakfasts and Cam told the waitress, as usual, "He'll have the *rye* toast please!" and watched Riley's face for the smile. I was fretting, running down loose ends out loud—*We still have to call the, Mink have you heard from the, Is our percentage confirmed for the*—but the others were in good moods. It was a soft blue day, warm for January, and our van had new tires.

"Send postcards remember," said Riley.

"You've only reminded me a hundred times," said Cam.

"Last time you didn't," he accused.

"Aren't you supposed to be back at college?"

"Next week," Riley said. "We have a long winter break."

"We'll put you on the list in Chicago," Mink said. "Don't forget to come."

"I won't!"

"Do we know where we're staying in Madison?"

"Not yet," I said, "but—"

"Lot easier if we still had a manager."

"If we still had a manager," I hissed, "we would be even broker, because that fucking plonker would have cleaned us out entirely."

Cam said, "But after this trip, we have to get someone. Too disorganized otherwise."

"What's disorganized? I booked twenty-five shows for thirty days. This is a well-oiled machine."

"You're the *queen* of booking!" purred Geck, leaning to lick my earlobe.

Cam closed his eyes.

In Scranton, Pennsylvania, we argued about food. Supplies from store versus sit down at restaurant versus drive-through. I, a despiser of all hamburger-related ingestibles, vetoed drive-through. Mink said a supermarket would save us money and Geck said supermarkets were too depressing.

"Let's decide by cephaleonomancy," said Cam. We waited for the definition he would supply: "Divination using broiled ass's head."

"You are a strange person," said Geck.

"We've passed like ten donkeys in the last hour," Cam explained.

Geck said, "Is a donkey the same thing as an ass?"

In Rockford, Illinois, P.I.T. stood for Private Indoor Terrain and was downy-chinned boys and their skateboards in a cavern stinking bright of plywood. Across one of the half-pipes I sprayed our name, then the stars and stripes of our city's flag. After playing for a jolly throng and drinking fake absinthe from the passed-around horn of a giant animal somebody claimed had been shot in Africa, we laid our sleeping bags at the top of a ramp. In that boy-built skatepark, falling to sleep in a row on wheel-scarred wood, I trusted deeply that things would be all right: I had my tribe to surround me, and thereby could not come to harm.

In Chicago, shy Riley could hardly bear the hissings of Can you get us backstage? Can you? I will *so* love you if you can. Their voices were a hot press *Can you? Can you?* and Riley hoped his head was shaking along with the rest of him. The pinprick in his forehead began to blare, a headache minutes away. When are they sound-checking? Are you going early? Can I come? He was shocked so many people knew who he was. It was a small college, but he didn't have many friends—wasn't *known*—or hadn't been, until the fliers went up and a slew of our fans got friendly all of a sudden. Maybe he wouldn't go. But he wanted to see us. He yanked up the hood of his windbreaker and left the dorm by the back stairs, happy it was raining because the umbrella further concealed him. The prickle in his forehead was bigger by the time he reached the club and stuttered to the guy on the stool who he was. A black tunnel with voices at the end, swivers of guitar, brisk thump of a drum, my voice going Coo, coo, coo! and Okay, how's that? When he emerged from the tunnel mouth, Cam was first to notice: Hey, Coyote! he yelled across the big floor and

Riley tucked his chin, shy, stroking the camera case dangling at his hip.

Riley had taken our picture for the *Purgastoria* cover. All four dressed in drugstore Halloween, black nylon long underwear painted with bones: Cam tall and planky; me whatever; Mink with movie-star teats pushing out the skeleton ribs; and Geck with his arms above his head, reaching for nothing.

I NOTICED THERE was no wine on the table. Water glasses sweated by the plates. My parents always drank wine at night; had Mert prodded Fod into giving it up? Did he have cancer? Did *she* have cancer? Did wine even affect cancer?

"This polenta is a masterpiece, let's be honest!" said Mert, bearing in a massive yellow mound.

"Smells delectable," said Fod.

"Pettle, would you move the trivet? Thank you. Now, everyone, I have some really nice goat's cheese, if you want to mix that in…"

"Did you guys run out of vino or something?" I asked.

"No," said Mert, "we're just not having any tonight."

"How come?"

She looked at Fod, who looked at Riley, who looked at the polenta.

"No particular reason. People don't always have to drink with dinner, so tonight, we're not."

"Well, but a particular reason must've made you choose *this* night not to serve wine, because every other night you do."

"Actually, a lot of the time when your father and I are on our own, we don't necessarily—"

Fod squinched his eyes. I believed my mother was not to be believed. I said, "Does someone have a disease and you're not telling us?"

"Oh, pettle, no! It's simply healthier for all of us to drink less."

"When you say *all of us*, do you mean—"

"You," said Riley.

"What?"

"She means it's healthier for *you* to drink less."

"According to who?"

My brother spooned a glistening dump of polenta onto his plate. "I asked Mert to not have wine tonight, so get mad at me, not her."

"Jesus, Ri, it's not like I'm an alcoholic!"

"But you drink a lot."

"Compared to who? You drink like a Baptist grandmother."

"Stop yelling," Fod said.

"Then you don't have to sleep on my couch anymore," said my brother.

"Is that a threat?"

"It's a promise."

I considered getting up from the table. I had done some storming out in my time, but I felt too lazy for it now.

"Who wants broccoli?" asked Mert, holding up the bowl.

We got a ride home from our father. Nobody talked at all. As we were climbing out of the car he said, "Sweet dreams, kids."

SOMETIMES WE WERE not alone. Unseen companions went where we did, reached their hands in. Tube blown, string broken, tire nailed on an empty highway. The companions had wooden legs and knocked gently, rattled softly out of rooms before you could catch them. I waited as long as I could stand before mentioning it to Cam. *This sounds crazy but…*but he did not think it was. He was good that way, a listener. I explained that the freakeries were friends of my sister. They spied for her, messed with us on her behalf. She had always been bossy; why not boss spirits? *On the third song, drop the latch in my sister's throat to kill her voice—she will panic!* I panicked. Fell away from the mic, spat foam, yelled unheard at the light-studded ceiling.

We'd had two meetings with the scout and it was all very vague, everything implied, many promises bandied about without a single one actually made; but I swallowed it. Cam was too suspicious—what was his problem? Couldn't he just be happy for once? We had a fucking Offer! But we *didn't* have one, he reminded me; there was no contract. No, but there would be, just as soon as we came back from tour. Scout's honor.

No longer would we sleep on kids' floors or in balcony motels; now it would be separate hotel rooms and my ego engorged to bursting and Geck on the covers of guitar magazines and—Cam didn't want anything to change that much. He wanted to keep us snug in a booth at the diner, together on the ripped seats of the van.

THE WARNING ACHE had started below my belly, though I wasn't due to bleed for two weeks. A hoof of cramp made my brain tell me we were eating too much—its reflex chorus—and I corrected my brain, No, we eat healthy and nutritious amounts, and it is normal for a uterus to discard its materials each month.

Did the bloodworm come to the army prisons?

The women soldiers wiped fake vagina blood on the men's faces. The men were tied to chairs, sore from beatings. It was bad blood, a pollution, worse for Muslim prisoners (said the radio) than electric shock: they were defiled. The worm said, I don't care if this blood is fake, I will come anyway! When a prisoner died in captivity, the worm ate his eyes.

The city was a toppled ship, the cathedral its pale prow. Leaden circles broke when they hit the sea floor. Broken bells heaped on my tongue; sun pricked my cheek where it touched the pane. Again the dungeoner was coming up Riley's street. *Again?* What was happening in his life that he needed so much of Mrs. Jones? I wondered what fortune he was getting. You will find the map! You will find your true love! The popular kids will die in their sleep!

Please have been sleeping. Please don't have felt a thing.

Did you wake them, little Coyote?

I knocked my forehead at the glass of the window that held the cathedral that sat on top of the city. Wrapped a broken-off piece of shoelace around my finger and sucked. Wake rhymed with lake, fake, and break.

When the dungeoner came out, he was walking slower than when he went in. Mrs. Jones had told him something he didn't like. He staggered into the street and almost got hit by a taxi whose horn was knife orange. Another car, nicer, waited for him to cross. On the other side of the street he lingered in front of the supermarket. Thanks to the hood I couldn't tell which direction his eyes were pointing, but from the way he was standing, they could have been pointed at me.

If you could meet the dungeoner, what would you say?

What would you say? repeated my sister.

I'd ask him what's wrong, and why is he getting his fortune told so much and can I—

Can you what?

Can I help him.

But he's a total stranger.

Not total, I've seen him before. Three times.

Three is black.

No it's green mixed with blue!

It's black.

No it's green! Like you!

I'm not green.

Yes you are.

Not anymore.

Then what are you?

Black.

But they didn't burn you.

I burned anyway. Under the ground.

Did it hurt?

No answer.

Sister?

Empty room.

Clench your teeth so the germs don't get in. Make your mouth a wall.

My brother padded in on his soft toes. "Who're you talking to?"

"Myself, as usual!"

"Coo?" he said.

"Coo," I agreed, noticing that his face had gone the particular gray it tended to go when he was bothered. "What's up, Coyote?"

"I'm—I'm—"

"*Yes?*"

"Mad," he finished, staring at the floor.

I waited.

"You haven't done dishes in three days. You *said* you'd be better about it!" He was still looking down.

"Right. I'm sorry. I've just been really stressed out."

"You're not even *working*!"

"Which is the source of my stress. I go into this panic mode where—"

"Don't explain. Just do the dishes."

"Yes," I said. "Totally."

"Also," he said.

"What?"

"You've been smoking in the shower."

"That is a lie."

"I could smell it, and there were two cigarette butts in the toilet, which you *didn't flush*."

"It's sad how anal you are," I said, instead of sorry.

I CALLED AJAX to propose myself as a babysitter. His kids liked me—*remember the movies at Christmas?*—and I wouldn't charge much.

I heard him breathing on the other end, wheezily, even though he'd quit smoking years ago.

"Well, what do you think?"

"I think," he said, "that a person with even below-average intelligence could reflect upon this situation for, say, five seconds and realize that a man who is unemployed does not need to hire a babysitter."

"Oh," I said.

"Not trying to be rude here, but, *hello.*"

"Right," I said, tugging at the rubber band.

"I HAVE TO pee," said Geck. "Can you pull over?"

Cam, at the wheel, said nothing.

Geck bellowed, "Have to pee!"

Still nothing.

"Pull over," I said.

"We stopped twenty minutes ago," Cam said.

"I didn't *need* to then."

"You'll have to hold it."

"I *can't*. My urinary glands are extremely sensitive." Geck waited, then added: "I could spray the back of your head."

"Yeah," Cam said, "I'm sure you'll do that."

Geck rolled down the window, knelt upright on the seat, unzipped, and carefully maneuvered his pizzle out the window.

Tribe is from the Latin *tribus*: originally, a third part of the Roman people. We were his people, even though he hadn't been with us long, and even though he peed out car windows. He played the guitar so weirdly well that we were going to get a deal. An actual one. With a major.

We sheltered from morning sun in a doughnut shop. I asked Mink for aspirin—cramps bad that day—and Mink said anyone who ate as much aspirin on her period as I did should see a doctor about it and Cam said, "Didn't you know she was born with an abnormally large uvula?"

We were always near each other's bodies. Bed to bed, couch to floor, front seat to back, sleeping close. We learned each other's sounds: Mink's humming, my tooth grinding, Geck's dream-moans, Cam's chirrupy snores. Whenever one of us let fly, the smell went straight up the others' noses. Cam's voice went softer when he talked to me *Throw me that ashtray* and brisker when to Geck *This pedal is crap, why'd you buy it?* (Uncle Seven once said, out of the boys' earshot: Your outfit's got itself a bit of an alpha male problem, doesn't it?) I knew how to dress their coffees—Mink black, Cam light, Geck light and sweet—and laughed at myself at the counter of a dirt-child café in Cleveland for being so moved by this knowledge. What is the big fucking deal, I told myself, giving our orders to a knife-collared boy; and yet knowing how they liked their coffees was a way of being family. It was like family how Cam and Geck, from the beginning, bickered worse than brothers and how Cam and I, by the end, weren't speaking at all.

"WHY ARE YOU whispering?" I asked the night phone.

"Because he's *here*… sitting like four feet away…"

"I can't really hear you."

"…!"

"Mink, I cannot hear a fucking word you are saying."

"I'm at work," she hissed. "I think you-know-who is using again."

"More than drinking?"

"It's—"

"What?"

"It's that—"

"Come again?"

"That *skull* look!" she sputtered. "He *has* it."

"Okay, drama."

"I'm *not being dramatic*."

"Are his eyes pinned?"

"I can't tell," Mink said. "He won't look at me. He's going to kill himself one of these days."

"Maybe so."

"*Maybe so*? Don't you give a fuck?"

"I give a small fuck only," I told her. "I mean, it's on him, right? He's a forty-year-old man."

"But he's our friend," Mink said.

"Then drive him back to treatment yourself," I said.

IN THE BLACK muffle of a motel room, a freakery reached its claw to my throat. Sent by my sister, the claw was moist; it wore her sweat. *Like a washcloth.* Its orders were to kill me, because she wanted me brung down to her where we could play. Cadmus, what will become of me? Now pull off my sheet. (But you're naked.) Pull it off. (But then I'll see your—) Pull it! (I see your—) You spent years looking, never found.

In Milwaukee, Wisconsin, some children resembling elves lived in a falling-down castle of a house, all turrets and rickety stairs. There were so many extra rooms that some sat empty, their walls rucked with old paint. The elves' elfin band was opening for us that night, just as they had when we'd come through town two years before. That first time, Cam had the flu and Mink had only recently joined us so was still fucking up her parts, but the elves loved us anyway and insisted we stay over. In the morning their singer brought a mug of sugared coffee to each of us, asleep in far-flung parts of the castle. He said sorry for waking us but added, You guys have such a long drive today I didn't want you to be late! and so we loved the elves back, and were happy to see them again, now, in the castle whose slate roof groaned with beer-scented snow.

It was the same body—a little hairier and harder-skinned, but still Cam. We were at the top of the castle, the attic room. He'd known where to look. Hi, I said. Hi, he said. Bare-shouldered in the sleeping bag we seemed younger, like our old selves who had kissed in the basement of Observatory Place. With the tip of his nose he grazed the tip of mine.

He was in me again.

He was too soon. "Fuck, sorry!"

"It's okay," I whispered.

He reached across my stomach for the lighter on the floor.

The air on our faces was cold. Somewhere below, Geck was shout-singing a nursery rhyme. The beer factories clanked and hummed. Cam licked the face of the sailor. Bit very gently the tail of the serpent as it bled into the doll's mouth. Snagged his tongue on the scars under the paint. I dragged my big toe up his calf, and could not wait to do it again.

ALL IS NERVOUS with him now I catch him looking at breakfast and look is like from high school—and did I even want to? yes but no but yes but why did I want to is the worry: is it horniness or is it really wanting to? because he hasn't been up there in quite a few years. He looks at me like telepathy but I'm not getting it, what message C? is it I want to again! or Let's forget it ever happened! Oh C why now—but, OK, I was there too—reminded me of ancientry hiding in the basement under my family listening to creaks and coughs getting ready for bed, we'd be so quiet fucking without noise since floor was thin and pipes were echoey. What the fuck I feel half-happy. Do you?

NEXT TO HIM in the backseat on our way out of Milwaukee, I couldn't stop smiling. Our thighs pressed in secret. The air was yeasty. The whole freeway as it curved past the factories smelled sour, and I loved the smell because it meant Milwaukee, which meant Cam's body reopened to me, pushing itself back into the space it had made when we were sixteen. He packed a new pack on his palm and yelled at Geck for going too slow in the left lane and I stared at his cheek, red from the razor, and at his grimy neck, wondering when I could kiss them next.

BUT WHAT IS supposed to happen now? If I break up with G he might leave us and where will we be? High chance of non-success without him. The Offer will get revoked. Watch me and C stop sleeping together like the <u>week</u> after we get home but G's already quit and we are cricked and Offerless.

THERE WAS TIME for one game before heading to my interview at the Christian-owned bookstore chain. This one was an old favorite. Controls cool in my fingers, I hunkered down. Plank over moat: you entered the castle. Somewhere, deep within, behind oak panels, through slimy passages, past trick-locked doors and manticores, he waited. His mouth was ready, wet and rosy, hiding a skillful tongue. He heard your boots floors above, knew you were coming, started to rub himself—and with his every sucked whine, you hurried faster to crack the locks, slide the bookcases, kill the little house dragon with a flung ax. When you found him, he would bend to your wrist, licking, licking, catching the rubber band on his teeth.

The man in the space helmet stood at the bus stop. Without looking at his face I dropped a bill into his can, and with this gesture warded off my embarrassment that the man slept on boxes while I did not—my throat filling, at the deposit of a hundred cents, with all the remorse to be found in pity, and I ordered my eyes to look back at him where he leaned against moss-veined brick, humming, counting coins.

The bus aisle was blocked by someone with a huge camera on his shoulder and another guy wielding a white umbrella. The news team? But if something TV-worthy had transpired, the bus would not be traveling its normal route. I strained to see what they were shooting. The bus driver, at my elbow, made a sound between throat-clear and horse-whinny and said: "Everybody gotta be a celebrity."

"Is that a celebrity?" I couldn't make out anything beyond the huge sweatpanted buttocks of the cameraman.

The driver shrugged. "I personally never saw him before."

When we rounded a corner sharp enough to throw the cameraman to one side, I finally glimpsed their subject: Jupiter, fly-eyed, wearing a suit made from what appeared to be tinfoil. His recently gauntened body lay in model pose across two plastic seats, and his hair, greased into an arrowhead, was flashing hectically in the umbrella light.

I turned back toward the bus driver, ready to disembark at the next stop.

"*Quinn?*"

Fuck.

"Hold on a second, boys," he said.

"We can take five," said the cameraman.

"Quinn, what's *up!*" shouted Jupiter. "Get over here."

"Hello!" I said gaily, squeezing past the other passengers. "Didn't realize that was you."

"Yeah, I know, kind of a demented place for a photo shoot, but they wanted to do a series where I'm in my old haunts. Like, this is the bus he took to get to work—this is the bar he used to drink at—"

"Because he, I guess, no longer takes the bus."

Jupiter smiled and I noticed some lipstick on his teeth, which I did not alert him to. "So how are *you*?" he said. "Tell me everything."

"Well, I'm—"

"You ever run into Geck? You know, he opened for us kind of recently. What a fucking disaster. I don't know what Lad is still doing behind a drum set—he's got such bad carpal tunnel he can barely swat a mosquito—and Geck, man, I mean, come on, *seriously*?"

A beehived girl heaved in to dab Jupiter's face with a powder puff. As she withdrew, her shellacked hair hit me in the chin.

"I've never seen them play," I said.

"I just feel sorry for the guy. Somebody should tell him that his wares are way past their sell-by date."

"Ready, Jupe?" said the cameraman.

"Yee-ah," he said.

"Have a good, um, shoot," I said.

"For sure. And next time we play in town—" He straightened his foil collar. "I'll totally put you on the list."

Cam had hated him too.

After an unpromising interview with a woman wearing a lapel button that said "Spread the Good Word," I hurried back to Riley's to type out the message I'd been composing in my head: *Hi again. Want to go to the diner sometime for old time's sake? If you have time. If not, no problem of course.*

In Madison, Wisconsin, I pictured Geck finding out. Throwing a tantrum. *You fucking said he was only a friend!* Twisting yellow hair in his fist. *Well, you love-birds have fun without me.* The scout on the phone: If your guitar player is no longer on board, we might have a problem . . .

IN ST. PAUL, Minnesota, Cam said: "But I love you again."

My cheek twitched.

He nodded. We sat in the screeching sun of 10:00 AM

"Well," he said.

"Well," I agreed.

He got to his feet and pulled on his jacket and touched the pockets.

"Here," I whispered, throwing him my own pack.

Lacustrina never cried, nor did she bleed.
Her skin was made of water and her necklac-
es of weed. She loved to swim but preferred
to read. A boy ached to kiss her, in his hot
heart's shell, but Lacustrina said no thank
you and politely fared him well.

In the middle of nothing, under a cold-colored sky, we were headed for some little country town where a college was, a festival, a winter-wonderland deal with a bunch of bands and it paid well. It wasn't late but the sun was already setting, and we were hungry but not enough to stop. We had gummy bears and a loaf of bread on the van floor, rock with cold. We hadn't seen another car for more than an hour. All the Vikings, Geck said, must've gone back to Switzerland.

I HAD THE apartment to myself tonight since my brother, slow flower, might have been getting some sex. I was rooting for him. In fact I had sent up a prayer.

I sat in the push of the fan, lights off, watching. 7:42 PM: white female, big hips, fly-eyes. 8:48 PM: black male in baseball cap and hiking boots. 9:19 PM: white female, fake-fur jacket, peppermint tights. The dungeoner appeared a little after ten. I wondered if he was some high-school dragon plonker in love with the Middle Ages and without friends in the twenty-first century. The future he wanted: *You will get out of here. You will never see those popular kids again.* Or an also nerdy but older person, more genuinely eccentric, living alone in a dark apartment where he cataloged the pinned corpses of his collection (butterfly? rat?) and ate only food that could be delivered.

Well, frankly, I had nothing better to do. Downstairs, in the window of the takeout next door to Mrs. Jones, I settled in to wait. Should have brought a magazine. But how long could a fortune take?

I counted the white veins on pedestrians, and the lights in the sky.

Then he came out: stark-white, maybe a few years older than I was. Couldn't figure out his hair because the hood covered it, but he had freckles and his nose was pointy. His gaze veered toward the takeout. I watched it land on me. The eyes stopped. I didn't move. *If you asked the dungeoner why he wears a hood, how would the dungeoner reply?* I smiled, which I didn't ever do at strangers. Slowly, the dungeoner turned back to face the street, and walked away.

I hoped Riley was meeting with success. Pine, in her accountant's vest, might be saying, "I have cooked you some classics from my homeland," leading him to a table laid with brown and yellow foods. "Toad in the hole, garlic mash, baked beans on toast, fish fingers all in a line."

"Looks delicious," said Riley.

"You are the politest boy I've ever known," she said without looking up from the crumpet she was slicing.

Pine had probably done it with tons of boys back in England, figured Riley, and it was probably no big deal.

I'm sorry you never got to, sister.

Pine forked the crumpet onto his plate and asked, "Have you ever heard of the Strello mountain in Portugal? It has this lake where the remains of sunken ships allegedly float to the surface. But it's an *inland* mountain. Mysterious."

He shook his head.

"It seems like a place your sister might have liked. The one who—I mean, you once told me she loved a good shipwreck."

"Yeah, she did."

"We should go there," Pine said.

Riley stared at her. "Where?"

"To the Strello mountain."

"I…"

"I'm a good traveling companion," she said.

"I don't know if I am."

"You *are* kind of moody," Pine said.

"Shut up!"

"Well, you are. But I'd still go with you. I mean I'd—I'd very much *like* to go with you."

She was a lake dweller; he could kiss her. *Go on!* but Riley couldn't quite. He asked, "What if there are ticks in Portugal?"

"Then at the slightest itch, we'll tear off our clothes to see if dark pins have buried themselves in us." Pine laughed and nodded at the table. "Please, help yourself."

"I will," Riley said, "but first…"

"Mm?"

Every blood cell had run up to his face. He couldn't. He couldn't. *Yes, Coyote, you can!*

She was waiting.

He leaned forward and his shoulder knocked a plate into the saltshaker, which tipped with a clatter. "Oh, I'm sorry—"

"It's nothing," Pine said.

Go on.

"Well," he said, and lifted his mouth into the vicinity of her mouth. She bent to meet him.

WE'D ALL DONE it a thousand times before. You pride yourself on how well you drive in a compromised state. But now this one little time it couldn't quite be pulled off, because of the ice. There was a lot of ice. And trees like skinny black arms. Even in the sun such ice would have been hard to see, and this was night. After the show, we'd refused invitations to stay with adoring nineteen-year-olds because our next city was so far. If we hadn't refused, we would have woken up achy from dorm floor, and eaten eggs with the kids, and been on our way—late to the show, but all intact.

THE NEXT MORNING I called heartily from the couch: "That sure was a long dinner."

"Shhh!"

Pine was right behind him.

I looked up meekly from the tangled sheets. "Guten tag," I said.

"Want breakfast?" Riley asked.

"Depends on the selection. What are you—"

"Actually, it's a yes or no question. Yes, thank you for offering to cook me food, that's very nice of you! or No, thank you, I have to leave in a minute to go find a job so I can stop living at my brother's apartment."

Jesus. Maybe he *had* gotten lucky.

While Riley fried eggs, Pine reclined with me. I tried to think of a conversation topic. Kids were screaming their heads off in the street below, so I remarked: "Somebody should get a shotgun."

"Do you not . . . " she said.

"What's that?"

"Are you planning not to have children?"

"I don't know. I guess not. Probably not."

Pine smiled grandmotherily. "It isn't as if you're out of time just yet. You have a few years before you need to worry."

"Thanks," I said.

"No—that sounded rude—I'm sorry—I'm not very much younger myself, almost thirty in fact—I didn't mean to imply that—"

"I'm not offended." Although I was, a little.

Was I?

Not on the surface of my brain, no; but my throat had tightened when she said *before you need to worry.* I had gone for most of my menstruating life not thinking of babies at all. Majority of the last decade, nothing; and before that, nothing either, except after the crash, when I had believed my missed period meant I was going to have Cam's.

" . . . bring up a child in a city, you know?"

"What?"

"There are so many toxins in a city," Pine was saying, "I just don't know if I'd want to expose a child to them. Pollution, crime, billboards, rampant consumerism . . . I was raised in a village where I drank milk squeezed the same morning from a cow I'd named myself."

"Hmm," I said.

MINK SMOKED, AWAY from us, one shoulder against a tree. In the stabbing cold she was sweating. Her narrow eyes hung wider; the blue was brighter in them. She hummed and stared at Cam's cheek where it flattened into the window. All his blood had quit running. If you prodded that cheek it wouldn't flinch; if you pushed a tweezer under his eyelid he wouldn't cry; if you wrapped your fingers around his junk it wouldn't move. Did Cam have a big one? Mink had wondered from time to time, suspected he did. He was tall.

I stood with my face shoved into Geck's jacket. Us two, having our hugfest, our little moment; Mink would have spat on us, had she had any energy left over from leaning against the tree. Maybe she should start screaming too and somebody would come hug *her*. Then Geck was moaning about his leg—if it was even really hurt in the first place—Mink had her doubts.

"We have to start the van for some heat," she said.

Geck and I looked horrified at the prospect of getting back into the van.

"You want to go gangrene?" she asked.

She reached in to turn the ignition, but nothing happened.

Each of us tried pressing the gas pedal with one hand, twisting the key with the other.

"Hood's busted shut," Geck observed.

"Or else *what*," said Mink, "you'd fix the engine?

IT HADN'T JUST been alcohol I relied on to sing; it had been the colors. They'd shown me where to put my voice. I simply had to move it up—or down—to where a certain color was. If a note was wrong, the color would be wrong, and I wouldn't go to it.

In high school, Fod had memorized the periodic table with ease because each element was its own hue, audible on the wall. The colors were *helpers*, he'd explained to us in the garden, and we must not be afraid of what we saw or heard or smelled; but remember, other people might not understand. We didn't have to tell everyone we met.

"We shouldn't tell?"

"No, we can, but we don't *have* to," said my sister. "Right, Fod?"

"Right, pettle. Not if you don't want to."

It came from him, he said, and we would give it to our own children, or else it would skip a generation and our grandchildren would get it. Why didn't Riley have it?

It only wanted you two, Fod said. It was always referred to simply as *it*. Not until after she died did I learn the term *synesthesia*, which sounded like a cross between a crime and being put to sleep.

SISTER, DO YOU remember blood?

Two speeds: slow from your downstairs, quick from your up.

Monthly creeping red, the chunks and glistening bits, you cried for it to stop. Four days, I warned with satisfaction, maybe even *five*!

The bullet made a door and out out out it came, red water and brain.

Red was hardening to black on Cam's face; his head drooped weirdly to the side, like it wasn't attached right; his eyelids did not flutter; but otherwise he might've been asleep. None of the bluish pallor I associated with deadness had yet chilled his skin, which was pale to begin with, ours all was, a whole team of ashen people. I tried, through the whiskey sog, to feel sad.

I hadn't yet noticed his hand.

"**IF YOU HAD** only one leg, how would you get to school?"

"Mert'd drive me," said the oldest.

"Mert is dead."

"Of what?"

"Diploria."

"What does that do?"

"Shrinks your skin," said the middle, "until it's too tight for your body."

"Then Fod would drive me."

"No, he's in a mental institution because of gone mad after we lost the Super Bowl."

"Then Riley?"

The middle looked over at the youngest, who was guiding a Slinky down the front steps. "No, his penis got caught in a Ferris wheel, and he can't drive anymore."

"I'd buy a wheelchair I guess. This is a dumb one," added the oldest.

The middle snapped: "Then we won't play at all."

"No, we can play, just think of less dumb of a one."

"If it's so dumb *you* think of some because I'm not thinking of any more ever."

"Yes you are."

"No I'm not."

THE BLACK PLASTIC suitcase was packed neatly. I fingered his glimmie. Held up his gray turtleneck and smelled on it the pomade he used. Cam was the least decorated among us and had the fewest vanities; pomade was a rare indulgence. At home, he kept the black-orange jar on his dresser. The scream rose again, thrusting up, swallow, swallow, I would not scream. *Swallow, Quinn*!

Lights from the road. We all looked up, saw the lights slowing. Witnesses. Police. Breath-testers. Killer-arresters.

"We have to decide," said Geck, excited by the idea of police, "what our story is."

"There's no story," Mink said. "We just ran off the road and Cam was driving. And"—she took the last cigarette from her pack, which we eyed, covetous—"we are never going to tell anyone."

I nodded.

"Not even my wife?" asked Geck.

Mink said, "I doubt you're going to have a wife."

Rigor mortis had not yet set in, so Cam flopped in our clutch. The muscles gave no fight; the bones slid and sank. The britches he had put on that morning, navy corduroy rubbed thin at the knees, would have to be cut off by the mortician. The long-haired skin on his arms felt amphibian. And I saw his hand, or what was left of it: a red flesh-mash that brought to mind the body of the mother mole, with her seed-babies crushed inside.

Those lights had kept going, had not stopped. But more would come—

I raked Cam's hair, stiff with pomade and cold, into a more flattering slant. Purpling veins webbed his yellow eyelids. The pimple near his mouth he'd been complaining of, how it wouldn't give up no matter how many times he pinched it open, remained a fresh red; was it still growing? Does skin go on breathing for a time after the heart has quit? I stuck out my tongue to taste, but the pimple had no flavor.

The passenger-side windshield was a blasted star, glass torn by tiny veins. "We have to break the whole thing," Mink told us.

I watched her expectantly, my shaken brain not bothering to grope for the reason.

"Because Quinn doesn't have any cuts on her face," she said and pulled a shred off her lower lip. "It's easier to break the windshield than give her the right-looking cuts."

Mink pulled the ride stand out of the back of the van. It was the sturdiest piece of hardware, and sharp-tipped, and she handed it to me. I stood on the passenger side, raised the stand behind my head—a bulky spear—and ran the metal hard as I could into the eye of the star Cam's head had made.

I broke it on the first go, straight into the cracked eye while Mink pointed the flashlight. I didn't stop there: hut hut hut into the van's hood, ramming and denting, hoping to pierce through to the engine.

THE WHITE-VEIN PEOPLE sucked brain juice into their pockets, rushing. The good-suit people checked their watches, rushing. The spruce girls clicked little heels and tightened little scarves, rushing. The space-helmet man, propped against the mossy wall by the bus stop, hands balled in pockets, nodded at me. I nodded back but it felt forced, a mark of some conspiracy we didn't actually share. He was one of the hundreds of patients discharged from the mental hospital without further ado, thrown out to roam. They were distinguishable from the vets, who muttered less and wore army-colored pants and held signs.

I pretended to look for the bus but was watching Space Helmet's face, wondering what the bells on the sky told him.

The new owners had let art students mural the walls of the diner. One panel showed a line of blindfolded men in turbans, with scrolls labeled U.S. CONSTITUTION aimed like rifles at their heads; another had a row of mouths sewn shut with dental floss spooling from a box marked PATRIOT ACT.

In the velvety mists of high school, before mobile phones and the smoking ban, my parents had not been able to reach me and we'd sit at the diner for hours, finishing cups and packs, making fun of people's garb, while Mert paced her heels off on Observatory Place. *It isn't safe for you to be out until two in the morning.* But what could have been safer than boothfuls of children in a café where they didn't serve alcohol? "No guns allowed," I'd muttered when Mert screamed, her voice worst first thing in the morning. I had almost told her that Cam, in fact, sometimes brought a *book* to the diner and read it at the table, which was in my opinion boring and rude; but Mert would have approved.

He was already sitting down—at a table, not our booth—so I couldn't see if he had the dad-denim pants on. He wore a thick green professorial blazer, despite the heat, and smiled up at me like a receptionist. "How are you?"

"I'm fine," I said, sick at the thought of the next hour being like the pumpkin coffee, at which we had spoken of nothing important.

I waited until we had ordered to say: "Look, Cam."

His mouth twitched. "Yeah?"

"I apologize," I said.

"For what?"

"For the whole—the whole thing. The van. Your hand. The—the—the what we did after."

He pursed his quivering lips. "The framing, you mean."

"Well, no, just that we moved you—"

"So that the crash would be blamed," he said, "on me instead of you."

"It was Mink's idea," I blurted, like a child.

His eyelids fluttered, nearly closing, in what I took to be disgust.

"But we went along with it. I'm sorry. I'm really, really sorry."

"Okay, one of these is super hot, so be super careful, okay?" cried the waitress as she set down our plates.

"Thank you," Cam told her. He unrolled the paper napkin with his right hand, shook it onto his lap, and said: "Well, this looks good."

"Yeah," I said helplessly, peering down. I had ordered the menu item least likely to resemble flesh, fat, or blood: spinach salad. A rare foray into the vegetables.

It was strange to miss—so much—a person you were sitting right across the table from.

Lacustrina never let boys touch her downstairs, because she had no downstairs. At her belly button, a snake started.

Cam's oaky eyes squinted. He ran his thumb down the spine of his nose. "How's yours?"

"Mouthwatering," I said.

I wanted him to reach for my shoulders, starred and unstarred, and thumb my breastbone hard and say, "You couldn't have seen that ice—no one could have!" But he did not reach, did not forgive, and said only: "These eggs are a little hard."

I finished my glass of water, the only thing that would fit down my throat.

I watched Cam eat small squares of cut egg, one by one, before starting on the buttered toast.

"Why did you come back here?" I finally said.

"I was offered a teaching position."

"Yeah, but you didn't need to take it."

He put down the toast, brought the napkin up to dab his mouth. The wounded hand stayed in his lap. "I can assure you, it wasn't so that I would run into *you*."

"I can assure you, I didn't think it was."

"My father has cancer," he said.

"Fuck," I said.

"It's a chance to spend time with him."

"But you said—last time—you said your parents were doing well."

Cam shrugged. "They're not."

I was about to say *I'm sorry* but decided those were words Cam didn't need to hear again from me.

WIPE THE BLOOD down his face. Yes, like that. Good soldier. Make a red handprint. Tell him it came from your downstairs. Tell him he can't wash it off.

WE WERE WARM together at the table. The windows were black mirrors. Snack was milk tea and cinnamon toast. The radio played pink-quill music. My sister dipped her nose in the teacup and Riley folded a whole half of toast into his mouth and Mert said, "Pettles, don't greed."

The news, interrupting, said a plane bound for Florida had crashed into the Fourteenth Street bridge immediately after takeoff.

"Jesus," Mert said, leaning to turn it up.

The cause of the accident has not yet been determined. Freezing weather conditions may have been a factor. Investigations are under way.

"But are the people okay?" asked Riley.

The radio went back to music. Mert got on the phone to the Walkers, who had a TV. "Mind if I bring the troops over?" We ran next door, without coats.

I WAS SHAKEN awake into a tearing hangover. Riley's pea-green eyes blinked above. "You must get away," I whispered.

"But the dungeoner," he said.

"Get away."

"He's in Mrs. Jones's. Just went in."

"I thought she didn't open until noon."

"It's two thirty, Quinn."

"Why aren't you at work?"

"I took a personal day," he said. "You were making sounds in the night."

"I was?"

"And I thought you might be sick." He nibbled at a finger. "I think we should follow the dungeoner. Because I have a theory who he is."

"Who?"

"The robber. From the Walkers'. The boy who made Mr. Walker shoot? He's come back all these years later to apologize, even though it wasn't actually his fault she got killed, but he can't muster the courage so he just pretends to get fortunes when in fact he's watching my apartment."

"A convincing theory," I said.

"It could be true!"

"Yes, well, it *could.* Do you have any aspirin?"

He scurried off and I wondered, for the millionth time, why my brother was so nice to me.

I ate four tablets, creaked into sweatpants, and decided it was best not to look in the mirror. "Do you have sunglasses?"

Riley produced red ones that might have been given away at a children's water park.

"Any *other* sunglasses?"

"God, Quinn!"

"Sorry, sorry."

"We don't really have to follow him. But let's go for a walk anyway."

"A walk?"

He blinked. "It's good for the blood."

Quietly we went west, along the yawning mouth of the park, until we got to the Buffalo Bridge.

"If you could pick the bridge you jumped to your suicide from, which would it be?"

"Any in the world?"

"No," said the middle, "around here. Because you wouldn't pay to go to another country to kill yourself."

"I might," said the oldest.

"Mine would be the Key Bridge," said the youngest.

The middle rolled her eyes. "Okay, boring! I would pick the Buffalo. The best-looking and the longest fall."

The youngest had once been scared of the Buffalo Bridge, when he did not understand that the giant green animals at either end were stone and could not charge.

"I'd pick the Fourteenth Street," declared the oldest.

"Why?"

"So I could die in other people's watery graves."

"Maybe we should turn back," I said, longing for more aspirin. A roomful of aspirin. I nodded at the buffalo statue, huge above us. "Hideous fucker. Check out his beard. Wildlife shouldn't have beards."

"Only sisters," Riley said, smiling.

"I do *not*."

"A little bit you do. Some rogue hairs."

I reached up for my chin.

He stopped smiling. "Quinn, look."

"Yeah?" I stepped closer to the stone rail, expecting him to point out a beauty or an oddness.

"You need—" He cleared his throat. "You need to leave soon."

"I know, I *know*. I've been hunting. There just isn't anything cheap enough, unless it's way out beyond the reach of public transportation. And I'm not getting my license back anytime soon, so—"

"I mean you need to leave next week. By the end of next week."

I thumbed my wrist. "Is that a deadline?"

"I'm sorry. I know you're having kind of—kind of a hard time. But you can't keep staying with me."

"Wow."

"I'm *sorry.*" His mouth crumpled; his furry eyebrows scrunched.

I admired my brother yet again. He was taller, but not by much; I could easily reach the top of his head. I put my hand there and pressed down, wanting to give him a heat of okayness, solidity, love.

DON'T UNDERESTIMATE YOUR local library, Mert used to say. It was her favorite place to send us when our boredom was on her nerves. Squidlings in a row, she arranged her children from tallest to smallest. My sister held one hand in front and one behind, chaining us, and it was she who liked the library best. I hated her for liking the library and for singing in front of strangers the story of the girl who fell from a cliff and was a miner's daughter and drove ducklings. I used to wonder—when she broke into public song, or rocked back and forth on the floor—if my sister was going to end up an unbalanced person who had to be placed in supervised care. Riley and I would visit on the weekends, guiltily.

Black trees, black sky, arms of light on black road. I'd found a decent station, a wee-hours college show to keep me company while the others slept. I strained to see ahead. Lit cigarette after cigarette to stay alert. I had no company but the music, cutting in and out of static, and the occasional whimper of a girl reciting the playlist.

And here's one we really like. The runaway hit by... and "Dear Done For" started and I didn't want to hear it and I leaned to turn the dial and it was fast and fucked and white and—

She made us crash, my sister did, lonely and jealous down there in purgastory; she wanted company. She knew the song was about her, and *she* made the ice slick—and the tires not catch—and the road edge a steep incline instead of a field.

But her powers weren't accurate. I didn't die.

It wasn't enough to send the freakeries, was it? To blow out speakers in the middle of important shows? To break strings, spill bottles, claw my throat in the night? She had to have me all to herself. *You are Cadmus and I am Europa. You spent years looking, never found.*

I rolled over on the damp sheet and kicked off the blanket it was way too hot for.

Like a washcloth. My sister hadn't been mad by the time she fell asleep. Had she?

I shut my eyes tighter.

She hadn't been. *Had not.* She was pestered by the heat and happy there was no school the next day and smiling under her eyelids. She said how the heat was on us like a washcloth made out of bread, and I—dozy too—said, "That's gross."

"You have to switch places," Mink said. "Move Cam to the driver's seat."

So will you switch places now? Okay, but only this one time.

IT WAS MINK'S third outing with the latest guy, and her hopes had not yet been dashed. "He's *nice*," she kept telling me. "Just a nice, regular person."

"In other words, dull?"

"No! He's cool. I mean, cool in that he's not cool. He's not *trying*."

"Remind me what he does, again? Fireman?"

"Web designer," she corrected. "He's a grown-up."

"Have a marvelous grown-up time," I told her. "I'm taking the terror to dinner. Meli," I called over the roar of cartoon, "we're eating out."

No response.

Mink jogged over to shut off the TV. "Quinn has generously offered to feed you tonight."

The girl smiled up at us from the carpet. "Awesome."

"I was thinking Chinese," I said. "We can get pot stickers."

Meli shook her head. "Can we please go to You Hop, please?"

"Not tonight, bee," Mink said quickly.

"But I want You Hop."

"Well, you're not going there."

"But *why*?"

"Because you're not."

"But I want chocolate-chip pancakes."

"Then you can stay home," said Mink. To me: "Sorry."

"It's not her fault she likes them," I shrugged. "How about deep-dish pizza?" I would not let the bloodworm come. I would eat like a regular person. Hamburger nubs were not my sister's flesh.

"Oh, yes! Okay!"

A car horn. "Have a great time, beautifuls!" cried Mink over her shoulder.

It had crossed my mind to ask her if could I stay here for a little while. She'd have said yes, however reluctantly. But Mink was irrevocably responsible for the welfare of a small human being. She didn't need me on her couch too.

"Oh god Quinny! Come here quick!"

"You're not allowed to cause catastrophe on my watch," I shouted back.

"But spider! By the terlet!"

Last summer, in the park, when the girl had been reduced to spasms by a web hanging across our path, was the first time I'd regretted that a dad was not around—to brush the web back with his *powerful forearm* and boldly decree: Can't hurt you, sweetheart! Where could Mink have bought such a father? During her recent stint with a flower-shop manager, I'd noted that his voice was too high to qualify for the position. His forearms—slimmer than my own—had had little power in them. He'd played cards with Meli, but I wanted him to wield a knife. Slit the necks of encroaching wolves, laugh at their blood tracks on the snow, on his shoulder lean an ax for the wood. Meli's biological father had been a one-week stand whose name Mink had practically forgotten by the time she found out she was with child. He moved to Los Angeles before the baby was born. Meli had been told he was a good person, someone good who was far away now and could not live near them. That paltry line had, miraculously, sufficed. It wouldn't always. Soon she would start asking, *But who was he? How did you know him? Did you love him? Did he love you?*

I wadded up paper towels and slammed them down on the creature, telling myself not to be such a girl.

She whined, "But what if his brothers . . . ?"

"Then we'll kill them too. First, however, we have an appointment with hot cheese. Get your shoes."

"I'm wearing shoes," she pointed out.

THERE ONCE LIVED a girl who had lost a leg in a Ferris wheel accident and was unfit for all the jobs of work available to her. This girl could not pay the weekly attention required of her by law of the village where she resided. From her red hill she watched the ocean and longed to disappear under its waves where it made no difference if she had one knee or two.

AFTER THE ACCIDENT, and after the flight home from Minnesota, and after a plastic surgeon had tidied up the four holes on his hand, Cam left town. Nobody knew where he went. I called his parents' house and his mother told me Cameron preferred not to have contact and she would appreciate it if I didn't call again.

And when, after what seemed like forever, my period still hadn't come, I concluded I was pregnant. The pee sticks were negative, but those foggy lines are so hard to read in the first place and my blood kept not coming, not coming, same as in high school, only this time I rubbed my belly every night and whispered to the baby: *Grow well!* I didn't drink a drop of alcohol for three weeks. It would have Cam's black hair and height and smartness; it would have my, what, I didn't know—maybe the freckles—but most things, I hoped, would come from him.

THE HOSPITAL SMELLED sad. All hospitals were required to. The one in Minnesota had still been decorated, on the sixteenth of February, with paper Christmas trees along its salmon halls. This one featured a pamphlet tacked to an otherwise empty corkboard: DOES THE PERSON YOU LOVE MAKE YOU HATE YOURSELF? We were directed to a distant floor, the chemical dependency unit, a hall of smudge-eyed shufflers in gowns and a guy crying into the pay phone: "But you said—but you *said*—"

Geck's skin was a little gray, the acne scars more pronounced, but otherwise he looked good for someone who had almost died. His shirt was off, the sheet bunched at his waist; I hoped he wasn't naked under there.

He rasped, "Wow, my first visitors, other than those whose loins I sprang from!"

"Here," Mink said, thrusting forth the box of chocolates.

"Thanks, valentine."

"Why's your voice all . . . ?"

"They ram this tube down your throat," he explained, "when they're plucking you from the reaper's jaws. I don't remember the tube, but it still hurts like fuck, so I guess it happened. Awesome-town, let me tell you. Heart?" He held out the opened box. I shook my head, but Mink took a chocolate. She'd gone to the gym four times last week.

"So how long do you have to stay here?"

"It's like this fourteen-day program. Standard fare."

We stood uncertainly by his bed. He coughed and sipped from a plastic cup. Finally: "You just missed my nidget roommate. He's at group. Already tried to poach my wallet. I wake up from a nap, right, and first thing I see is his withered hand in my personal-items drawer— but anyhoo, you guys want to admire my cane?" Geck reached for the long stick leaning next to the bed. "This here is made from a bull's pizzle. I asked my mother to bring it to cheer me. She has no clue what it's made of. Other than my dad's and mine, I am pretty certain this is the only penis she's ever laid a finger on!"

"Don't talk about your mom like that," Mink said.

His belly and biceps were flecked with little white slashes. I'd seen stretch marks on Mink's bubs when she'd aired the dairy, and on my own thickening hips; but they were surprising on a guy-body. Sad white body, inflating, deflating, drawing on ever-shrinking puddles of strength to bounce back from years of chemical dousing. Body that had once put itself into my body. Sex with Geck hadn't been bad. He'd shown a lot of enthusiasm.

In childhood, he had not dreamt of being jobless, carless, and poonless at forty, overdosing in his parents' ranch house. The boy Geck had had more interesting plans for himself. A hot stripe ran from my ribs up my throat, opening at my teeth like a flower. I didn't want him to die. He might not have been the most luminous bulb in the chandelier, but he was a full-knit body of fibers and cells, skin that bled if you ripped it, hair that came out in the shower. He had a mouth that kissed well, even with its roan tooth. First time I ever saw the tooth up close I had laughed, and he'd said You're chuckling at my dental burden aren't you.

Now here he lay, pantless under a sheet, pretending to enjoy the piffle we'd bought at the hospital gift shop—acting unbothered by the fact that he was on a bed with metal sides. Well, *I* was bothered. A person could slide off the earth in one second, never to return.

Mink leaned back in a chair with the penis cane propped between her knees, clicking her long nails along its shaft. "So what happens after fourteen days? Outpatient again?"

"Uh, sadly, no." Geck coughed again and I handed him the water cup. "My counselor doesn't think I'm a *trustworthy candidate* for outpatient. Wants me to go to a halfway house—"

"Great!" we said together.

"In rural Pennsylvania," he hissed. "I'm supposed to get away from my usual persons, places, and things. But what am I gonna do all day, milk Amish cattle?"

"Think of it as a vacation," Mink said.

"Plus you're too old," I said, "for this crap. OD'ing is a young man's game."

"I'm young," he said irritably. "Look at my hair."

THE MIDDLE OPENED her notebook. "Here is the first question: If you were sentenced to death but could pick the method, would you rather be drawn and quartered or killed by necklacing, which is *a form of punishment used in South Africa by blacks against blacks thought to be government sympathizers by which a petrol-soaked tire is placed around the victim's neck and ignited*?"

"What's drawn and quartered, again?" asked the youngest.

"Where you get each arm and leg tied to its own horse and they all gallop in different directions."

"Oh yeah," said the youngest.

"Necklacing," decided the oldest, "because you'd die quicker."

The youngest had to agree.

MOST OF MY earthly possessions lay stowed underneath Observatory Lane, so there wasn't much to pack. Cigarettes—underwear—Octy—and the old notebook, in a ziplock.

"You found a place?" said Riley, barging in with Pine, who looked milkier than ever.

"Uh, yep!"

"Where?"

"Secret," I said.

Pine inclined her head Britishly. "Nice to see you, Quinn."

"And you." I rubbed my low back, ablaze from stooping. "How were the salt mines today?"

"The chief was in an extrarude mood," Riley said, "but I…"

"What's that?"

"I *remained sanguine.*"

"You guys making, um, any tea?"

They looked at each other.

"Only because—you sometimes have afternoon tea. And snacks."

"You want a scone," Riley declared.

"I could murder a scone," I admitted.

Pine said she would be happy to make some, if we had any flour.

"You really don't have to," Riley said.

"Great!" I shouted.

"Settled," she said.

I was starting to like her.

While she whipped up her batch, Riley watched me push small items into bags.

"I'll be gone on Monday," I said. "Five days before the deadline, incidentally."

"So where's the new place?"

"Told you. Secret. But I have a favor to ask."

"I can't lend you—"

"No!" I said. "Not that. I am only asking for a few hours of your time. A day's worth. Next weekend."

"For what?"

"A little road trip to bring Geck to a halfway house."

"Why do you need *me* to come?"

"Because you have a valid driver's license, and I do not, and I want to borrow Mert's car because Mink's truck is in the shop, and Mert is highly more likely to—"

"I have to think about it," Riley said.

"Cinnamon or ginger?" called Pine from the kitchen.

"Ginger," he answered before I had a chance to say cinnamon.

"IF THE MAN in the ice had taken the rope, would the lady's ghost stay mad at him?"

"No," answered the youngest, "because the lady would understand—"

"But what if she didn't," said the middle. "What if she was too angry that he got to live and she had to die?"

"Then she would haunt him," said the youngest.

"Haunt how?"

"I don't know."

"What particular freakeries would she do?"

"I don't *know!*"

The middle said, "How about wake him in the night with the feel of being poured with freezing water? Turn his lips blue like if he drowned? Whisper in his ear until he went lunatic?"

"But he *didn't* take the rope," said the youngest.

The middle nodded, sighed, and stood. She hadn't even bothered to open the notebook. That was their last game of Curious. Stopping was not decided or discussed;

in the remaining months of the middle's life, they simply never played it again.

OCTY NESTLED IN my lap while I played Wake Up the Sister. In the dark room, only the scrinkling television was alive; and on the screen was a screened porch; and on the porch you were sleeping. The fold-out couch was lumpy but you were fifteen, healthy and strong—you slumbered easily. Morning came. A coyote pup wobbled in on stuggy legs to tell you it was time to get up. Together you had to rouse the sister.

Most times, the sister was dead; but every once in a while she was not. One of the buttons allowed you to earn Anti-guilt points by not asking her to change sides the night before, and thereby dying in her place. The points clicked up in a red dial on the screen.

If she was dead, you couldn't earn Anti-guilts or Virtues.

If she was dead, you could watch her in the afterworld trying to get strangers to play Cadmus and Europa.

WITH THIS VOYAGE, my brother and I were flouting family law. Never in the same car for any trip longer than half an hour. But Mert and Fod did not mention the flout; instead they encouraged Riley to honor the speed limit, especially once we reached Pennsylvania, whose state police were notorious.

"Thanks again for the car," I said.

"Just bring it back in one piece," said Fod. "And your brother does all the driving. Not you or—or the junkie."

"You *know* his name."

Riley put a hand on my arm and said, "Don't worry, Fod" with the authority of an elder sibling.

He double-parked in front of the diner. "Get us a couple of coffees?"

Sex—if he had, in fact, been having it—was making him kind of bossy.

In line, I glanced at the corner booth.

"All right, Riley Coyote." I secured the to-go cups on the dashboard. "Are you prepared to hit the countryside?"

He nodded. "What's a halfway house, again?"

"Where drunks and drug addicts learn to be satisfied with low-paying retail jobs."

"And how's *your* new house?"

"Basement room," I reminded him.

He smiled into the steering wheel. "How's your basement room?"

"Dank," I said.

"Is Ajax letting you stay for free?"

"For a month. After that, he said, he's charging rent. But I'll figure something out by then. I have a whole month."

"You'll figure something out," Riley echoed, ever staunch.

We got Mink at the sitter's where Meli was throwing a tantrum because she wanted to come with us. She'd accused her mother of *insufficient travel chances.* "She actually used those words," Mink said, clicking her seat belt.

At the end of his parents' driveway, Geck waited on a duffel bag from whose mouth poked the handle of the beloved cane. He stowed the duffel in the trunk and heaved himself into the backseat with a huge foil-wrapped platter.

"My mom made us some stuff for the road," he said. "Two kinds of cookie and one of brownie."

"That was nice of her," Riley said.

"Sugar is another white devil," Geck muttered. "Perhaps the most insidious of all."

I asked if he had the directions.

"Drive toward the cows and the people who use buttons instead of zippers."

"Pardon me?"

"*Yes*, I wrote them down, do you think I have wet brain *already*?"

He tore off the foil and we sampled his mother's efforts. In our van we'd had red chips, gummy bears, iced-up bread. Everything, then, had been icy. Now it was humid as hell and the air-conditioning in my mother's car was not what you'd call working well. Mink's face in the rearview looked slathered with petroleum jelly.

"Quinntanamo," said Geck, "if I hate this place, will you guys come rescue me?"

"You have to give it at least two weeks," I told him.

"Two weeks is long."

"But shorter than death," Mink said.

"We aren't lost."

"But we are," said Riley.

"We're *not*."

"I think we should ask someone," said Mink.

"Who," said Geck, "that tree?"

"We're *fine*, people—we're just on an alternate highway."

"This isn't a highway," my brother pointed out, "it's a dirt road."

"Shut up, Coyote, I know what I'm doing."

He added, in a whine: "You shouldn't even be driving."

"No one's going to find out."

"You lost your *license*."

I snapped, "You see any policemen around?"

"I need to release urine," Geck announced.

At a truck stop, he ordered his final beer. Mink reminded him it would be all the harder, with the taste in his mouth, to endure sobriety in West Butt Hollow; he said, "You don't say." The TV above the counter flickered with footage of tanks. Geck raised his bottle and Riley clinked it with a can of lemon-lime.

Mink read aloud from the place mat, where horoscopes were printed: "Sagittarius:" (Riley) "*You are embarking on a journey into new and exciting territory, whether geographical, spiritual, or sensual. Protect yourself from the dangers that attend this path but do not be afraid of the path itself.* Aquarius:" (me) "*Fences ask the nails to mend them. Bridges ask the water to run beneath them. Leo:*" (Geck) "*You should nourish your sense of humor today and learn some new jokes. There is a fair chance that you will win something by entering a contest. This could be a contest where you submit your own work of art, a funny jingle or poem or perhaps an insightful drawing.*"

Our sister had been a Leo too. I said to Riley, "She'd be turning thirty-three. What would she be doing, you think?"

"Mmm"—he slurped soda—"starting to have some kids?"

Those nieces and nephews, begging me for guitar lessons.

"Aren't you going to eat your…?"

"It's not cooked enough," I mumbled.

"Have some of my eggs, then," my brother said.

"I don't—"

"Quinn, come on." He hoisted half his omelet onto my plate. "At least a few bites, okay?"

I nodded.

A mouthful of pennies was a bullet.

It wasn't that the worm had gone. The worm had not gone. But it was quieter. I knew it could, at a moment's notice, tunnel in and raise up its blood-thick head; but it had not been huffing me quite as often. Its olfactory glands, with old age, were feebling.

The two in back slept, mouths open, Geck's forehead on Mink's shoulder. Riley steered with his hands at ten and two. The sky was a mess. Storm coming? I wouldn't have minded a storm. Earth soaked. Trees bent. Leaden circles breaking on the air.

My sister had smelled like trees and said she would pluck her eyebrows (the furriest in the room) but never did. She'd thought she might be a genius—confidence hadn't yet been sucked out of her—but also believed feelings were more important than facts. What does the brain matter, she had asked me and Riley, compared with the heart? The men who looped yellow tape around Edinburgh Lane had shoveled her spilled brain into a bag.

Between my hips, where the eggs lived: a little heave.

I'm sorry.

I know.

"Who are you talking to?" my brother asked.

"The forgiveness department," I said.

Giant hills ridden by giant trees; long spaces of water that I couldn't tell if were lake or river; and bruisy clouds. All the colors were dark: blues, greens, grays, browns, each hue muted and low to the ground.

"It's grummy out here," Geck complained.

"It's beautiful," Riley objected. "I think it's like a painting."

"Well, happy day for you." Geck sniffled. "Where am I going to be living, a Christmas tree farm?"

I pictured him red-nosed in December, tying evergreens to people's cars. "Maybe you'll finally morph," I said, "into the earthling you're fated to be. The lavender harem pants and Kokopelli-embossed belt have patiently waited, now to have their day in the sun while you tend bok choy outside your geodesic dome."

"Thank you," he said, "for making this worse."

ON JUNE 2, 1865, the American Civil War ended with General Edmund Kirby Smith surrendering his troops at Galveston, Texas. On June 2, 1953, England's Queen Elizabeth II was crowned in the first coronation ever to be televised. On June 2, 2004, it was twenty years to the day since she'd died. We were having family dinner and there had been no mention of why, although everyone knew why; and the last thing I wanted was to go; but Riley, with surprising firmness, insisted. He even met me at the subway mouth so we could ride the bus together. He told me on the bus that there was something we needed to do.

I assessed the table: only one set of glasses, brimming with water. So they were still a bit concerned.

Riley sent me a look: *Don't forget.*

We ate for a while, chomping and murmuring, and I started to think dinner might end before it happened. My brother's face was turning gray and red. His sweet lips jumped in their wet casings. He wanted to do it—I watched him want to—but he could not. The lips just kept jumping.

I was oldest. So I would.

"More asparagus, pettle?" said Mert.

"No thank you," said Riley.

"I miss Ant," I said, loud as I could.

The parents, hit, stared down; and the brother smiled.

Antonia. Ant. Oh. Ant-o. Afraid of pimples and in love with her notebook and could smell in a forest if a wolfberry grew.

I took a large bite of mashed potato, curious what would happen next.

Just quiet.

Then Fod whispered, "I miss her too."

"Antonia," insisted Riley.

"Antonia," said Fod.

"Antonia," said Mert, clearing her throat. "I miss her every single day."

"If nuclear war, would you rather be at home and die immediately, or at the beach where we would boil in the radiated waves but have a few last minutes to say our goodbyes?"

"Goodbye to who?" asked the youngest.

"Each other," said the middle, "and Mert and Fod. Like last words. I might plan mine out beforehand."

"I know mine already," said the oldest. "See you in hell!"

"I'm not going there," said the middle, "I'm going to purgastory."

"How do you know?"

"Because I just do," she said. "I am more of a purgas-torial person than a hellish."

"I am too," said the youngest. He would ask their mother later where it was.

Acknowledgments

A portion of this novel first appeared as "Pick the Method" in *Keyhole*. I'm grateful for generous support from the Djerassi Resident Artists Program, the Lower Manhattan Cultural Council, the MacDowell Colony, the Millay Colony, the New York Foundation for the Arts, and Yaddo. For their encouragement, insight, and help, I thank Heather Abel, Zelda Alpern, Kate Blackwell, Liz Brown, Michael Caines, Lila Cecil, Jennifer Firestone, Jocelyn Heaney, Noy Holland, Felix Jakob, Allison Lichter, Eugene Lim, Kisha X. Palmer, Shauna Seliy, Emilie Stewart, Natasha Wimmer, and the excellent people at Tin House Books: Lee Montgomery, Tony Perez, Meg Storey, and especially Nanci McCloskey. Special thanks to my dad, Nick Zumas, for telling me his story. And to Luca Dipierro, the love of my life—ti amo come un faro ama il mare.